THE DOCTOR'S SECRET

Nigel Blake is a busy and popular doctor, who finds it easier to communicate with his patients than with his wife Carolyn. Having given up her nursing career, she is frustrated by domesticity and the lack of emotional warmth in her marriage, so when Nigel takes on Max Faber as a partner in his practice Carolyn responds to Max's obvious admiration. It becomes clear that Nigel and Max knew each other in the past, and when Dr Anita Benson arrives in the neighbourhood the mystery deepens. It seems as though Nigel and Carolyn's marriage may not survive the secrecy...

THE DOCTOR'S SECRET

The Doctor's Secret

by

Sonia Deane

Dales Large Print Books
Long Preston, North Yorkshire,
BD23 4ND, England.

British Library Cataloguing in Publication Data.

Deane, Sonia
    The doctor's secret.

        A catalogue record of this book is
        available from the British Library

        ISBN   978-1-84262-572-9 pbk

First published in Great Britain in 1967
by Hurst & Blackett Ltd.

Copyright © Rupert Crew 1967

Cover illustration © Maggie Palmer by arrangement with
P.W.A. International Ltd.

The moral right of the author has been asserted

Published in Large Print 2007 by arrangement with
Rupert Crew Limited

Dales Large Print is an imprint of Library Magna Books Ltd.

Printed and bound in Great Britain by
T.J. (International) Ltd., Cornwall, PL28 8RW

1

Carolyn looked at the clock. Nigel was already an hour late. Who, she muttered to herself, would be the wife of a doctor? In that mood of exasperation, she bounced through the hall and into the kitchen, deciding – even before looking in the oven for about the tenth time – that the chicken would be ruined.

At that moment, she heard Nigel's car racing up the short drive and braking at the front door. That meant another patient or he would have gone straight into the garage, she thought rebelliously. For all that, she ran to greet him, hearing him say as he flung his coat over the nearest chair, 'I just can't go on like this.'

'That,' she retorted, 'makes two of us.'

'It's freezing out; the roads are skating rinks.' He stopped abruptly, her words suddenly registering. 'What do you mean, "that makes two of us"?'

'I'll tell you when I've fed you.' She hurried to the kitchen. He, brows puckered, went into the cloakroom.

When the meal was on the table, the chicken carved, they looked at each other with an inquiring uncertainty. Carolyn thought how tired he looked: he thought how attractive she was – almost as though seeing her for the first time. Her small, delicate features were framed by soft, yet thick, chestnut hair and her eyes glowed, despite their expression of faint challenge. They ate in silence apart from a few commonplace utterances until, as he finally put down his knife (rejecting most of the cheese on his plate), he said, forcing a note of lightness, 'Well! Now I'm fed – perfectly fed.'

'Let's talk in the other room.'

There, they settled in their usual chairs which were drawn up to a flaming fire.

'You have to go out again?'

'Mrs Martin started just before I left the nursing home.'

'Oh.' Carolyn felt mean. She had been worrying about time and an overcooked chicken. Mrs Martin had already suffered the loss of a son of ten who had been killed in a street accident. The second child, a girl, was stillborn.

'How is she?'

'Brave. This has just got to be right.'

'It will – you're her doctor now.'

His smile lit up his attractive, sympathetic face. He had the ability to inspire courage and confidence and was dedicated to his work. 'What did you mean just now? Not that I blame you for getting sick to death of the waiting.'

'We all get sick to death of things at times... What did *you* mean?'

'I meant...' The telephone rang. He answered it instantly. 'Yes, Sister. Right away.' He was out of his chair almost before replacing the receiver, talking as he hurried into the hall and dragged on his coat. 'What I said had nothing to do with Mrs Martin.' His gaze met hers. 'Won't you go across to the Merrimans?'

Carolyn shook her head. 'I'll keep the bed warm. Drive carefully,' she added on a note of breathless anxiety as she opened the front door to let in a blast of icy wind. A second later the car vanished, but she could hear the faint throb of its engine on the main road.

The house was suddenly still and empty. The evening no longer held any promise. Midders could take an hour, or all night, and she was afraid that in the case of Mrs Martin it might be protracted. Despite this, Nigel would lose himself in his work, time meaning nothing more than the satisfaction derived from the task.

Carolyn cleared the table of its debris and then stared down at the sink. Her thoughts shuttled between Mrs Martin, Nigel, and her own distaste for washing up. Sinks! They seemed so much worse on these occasions. Or was she tired of being the wife of a doctor? A wife trying to fit in meals at impossible hours and never being able to plan ahead with any confidence. She picked up a saucepan which was full of water, knocked it against the draining board, and poured the contents partly on to her feet and over the floor. The telephone rang at that moment. Probably, she told herself furiously, some woman complaining that she was constipated – a not unusual happening at the end of the day, or even during the night. A grating, tart voice greeted her. Mrs Wilder – the Practice Horror.

'Good evening, Mrs Wilder. Can I help you?' (If only the wretched woman would leave the district.)

'I must see Doctor Blake at once. It's very urgent.'

It was always urgent! Carolyn explained that a visit was impossible but, if necessary, she would telephone the Emergency Service.

'Emergency Service,' the voice snapped back. 'I do not want some strange doctor.'

Carolyn managed to sound patient. 'Then I will get my husband to call on you in the morning.'

'The morning will be too late. I just know I'm starting a cold and I have a very special party tomorrow night. Your husband knows exactly what I might need. This really is tiresome.'

Tiresome. Carolyn was thankful the line went dead at that moment. *Starting a cold.* The sink looked worse than ever as she returned to it. Thoughts tumbled over in her mind... It was now nearly ten o'clock. She knew what it would mean to Nigel if anything should go wrong... Mrs *Wilder.* Emotion, anxiety, found release in an up-surge of temper which died on the breath of fear. The later Nigel was the worse the roads would be. She went to the front door and opened it, shivering as she did so. There was no moon and the darkness seemed like a black backcloth on an eerie stage. Every sound was magnified as she listened, hoping to hear Nigel's car. There was never any mistaking his swift gear change as he turned off the main road into the short lane in which their house stood. One consolation was that the nursing home was not more than half a mile or so away. The cold bit into her and she shut the door and went back to the sitting room. Almost immediately the telephone rang and Nigel said, 'I'm just having a coffee... Yes, so far. I must stay here.'

He was called at that moment and seemed to drop out of her world completely. Having been a nurse herself before she married, Carolyn appreciated the excitement behind the concern; the comradeship associated with the team work of doctors and nurses. She wished she might be a part of it all.

There was a loneliness about waiting which brought isolation. Automatically, she tidied the room, placed the guard over the fire and decided to go to bed. As she reached the foot of the stairs she looked across the hall, and while it was attractive she knew that, to her, it lacked life. Her thoughts became layers of cloud rifting through a grey depression. What had Nigel meant by, 'I can't go on like this?' Was it work, or their life together? The objects of furniture in the hall blurred against the oak panelling. Colour dissolved into colour; the royal blue of the carpet, the golden lamp shades sending out the glow almost of a moon on a tropical night. She loathed the thought of going to bed alone, but he would be glad to find her there when he returned.

It was five o'clock when she heard his car and the front door open and shut. She called out to him, and as he came into the bedroom he said, 'A boy – both fine.'

A few minutes later he crept into bed – cold, weary. Within seconds his breathing was rather that of a child.

Carolyn lay awake, knowing that in a few hours there would be surgery. Cases of all kinds, and the next night another midder might start. It wasn't, she told herself, that she was lacking in sympathy for his patients, but that she cared for their life together because now it had become almost impossible. She wanted to be taken notice of – not in a nauseating way associated with glib compliments – but to be noticed as a woman. Yet she knew that if she were not there, he would notice her absence, and to be noticed only by absence was the final insult.

Unfortunately Nigel was an undemonstrative man, who found it almost impossible to betray emotion, or to convey the depth of his feelings. He detested insincerity and effusiveness, and his apparent lack of warmth concealed a passionate sensitivity.

At seven o'clock Carolyn struggled out of bed and went downstairs. It was not yet light, but the flush of a fading dawn remained in the sky and she stood at the window inspired by its beauty. The garden was white with frost which, in a brief while when daylight came, would glisten and create fairyland. Her heart lifted a little as she put the kettle on, made the tea, and took Nigel's up to him. At the sound of her voice he grunted, turned over, and went on sleeping. She hadn't the heart to rouse him again. Another half hour would do him good and it would not hurt a few patients to be kept waiting. He was always as punctual as it was possible to be, and made appointments for those most needy.

The winter sun was now pouring in as she returned to the hall and drew the curtains, changing both scene and mood. She drank a cup of tea and then returned to Nigel, who immediately stirred and said, 'Good Lord, what time is it?'

'Time for you to drink this,' she replied. 'I'm so glad about Mrs Martin, Nigel.' She spoke gently.

'So am I.' He handed her back the cup and jumped out of bed, heading for the adjoining bathroom. 'I've got a hell of a day,' he added.

Carolyn tried not to feel deflated. By the time she reached the kitchen Mrs Pringle, the daily woman, had arrived. Her gaze rested on Carolyn's face and she said instantly, 'Not much sleep for you last night, Mrs Blake.'

Carolyn smiled. Mrs Pringle could not be deceived over anything.

'Not a great deal – less for doctor.'

'I heard that Mrs Martin had a boy,' came the swift reply. 'Everyone was talking on the bus. Delighted we all were.' She nodded to her own thoughts, her round face beaming, her eyes bright. 'No one like Doctor Blake in these parts.' She took off her coat and hung it on is rightful peg. 'What you'll both be needing now is breakfast. Quickly.'

'Always quickly,' Carolyn agreed. She had no idea what she would do without Mrs Pringle, who managed to anticipate wishes, and work at the speed of a racing car – without creating any disturbance. Carolyn knew that in Lewes and its surrounding hamlets and villages, Nigel's name was synonymous with skill and integrity, and what might be even more difficult to find – compassion.

Breakfast appeared in the dining-room just as Nigel rushed down the stairs. Mrs Pringle oozed satisfaction as she said, 'I know we don't discuss patients, Doctor, but we are all so glad about Mrs Martin. We said she would be all right the moment she transferred to you.'

Nigel glanced up from the appetising bacon and eggs.

'Thank you, Mrs Pringle.' The, 'I know we don't discuss patients', appealed to his sense of humour. That over, he ate at the rate of someone starving who was afraid the food would be taken from him.

The door bell rang at that second. Surgery. He glanced at his watch. 'All I hope is that I don't have any crazy ones today. Not in the mood.'

Carolyn made no comment, but when, after an hour and a half, he strode into the sitting-room, she said, 'Obviously there was a crazy one.'

'Hair,' he said abruptly. 'Hair! Her life is being ruined by it. She lives in curlers, can't go out to dinner, or entertain her husband's friends, and can I do anything about it? Any minute now I'll open a hairdressing salon.'

Carolyn knew his mood, but would love to have told him that to a woman her hair was almost an emotion, and that her first reaction to any invitation was 'How is my hair? Can I get to the hairdresser, or can I afford it?' The man always thought that she looked at her best just when she was going *to* the hairdresser, and her hair hung lank and greasy. But, on a very special occasion, and when he wanted to present her to his friends, it was a very different matter.

'I must get to Mrs Martin,' he said as though talking to himself.

Carolyn followed him into the hall. She knew that the handy-man-cum-gardener-cum-driver would have already brought the car to the door. She waited, wondering if he would make one personal remark amid all the instructions she knew he was about to give.

'Get Mrs Weeks on the phone and tell her I shall be late in calling. She fusses. Oh, yes... Doctor Sims. Remind him of those X-rays; he promised them for this morning.'

Carolyn's calm held the quietness which precedes thunder, 'And have you your list of calls for this morning?'

He fumbled in his pocket.

She handed him the list. He grabbed it rather like a child taking a sweet.

'Will you be in for lunch?'

16

He had reached the front door by this time and answered, 'No … have to be at Alfriston to see old Mrs Grayson.'

For the first time in their married life, Carolyn did not follow him to the car. She stood in the doorway and watched him get into the driving seat. He wound down the window on his left and spoke through it. 'I shan't be home tonight – I mean not until late. Committee meeting at the hospital.'

'After your clinic?'

'Yes. Oh, tell Mrs Clark that I've left her instructions for this afternoon.'

Mrs Clark was the part-time secretary who worked for three hours in the afternoons.

The car raced down the drive and was lost to sight. Carolyn shut the front door and walked into the sitting room. She was angry with herself. To expect Nigel to think beyond his work at that particular time was childish, even unforgivable. But the defect did not make her any less human, or her emotional need less great.

Mrs Pringle came in, saying cheerfully, 'Now for a fire.'

Carolyn felt that her thoughts must be flashing on a large screen. She was conscious of Mrs Pringle's overt glances as she cleared the ashes, stacked the wood, and then put a match to what became a blaze.

'Nothing like a fire,' said Mrs Pringle, half to herself.

'Plus central heating,' Carolyn murmured mechanically.

'The grocery order,' Mrs Pringle prompted.

Grocery! Domesticity! The monotonous daily round.

'I'll make out the grocery list,' Carolyn said, sitting down at her writing desk which stood in an alcove, where a high window allowed the sun to cast its pale shadow. She felt like a clock that had been overwound to a point where the main spring had broken. The telephone rang incessantly and she answered it automatically. Patients wanting appointments when they knew Nigel was at the hospital (where he was a consultant gynaecologist), and that any emergencies could be seen by Doctor Hodder with whom he had a reciprocal agreement. Patients pleasant and charming; patients like Mrs Wilder who imagined that their cough, or their backache, should take priority even over the dying. As Carolyn replaced the receiver on what she fervently prayed might be the last call, a car came up the drive. She ran out into the hall and opened the front door, delighted, as she exclaimed 'Freda!'

Freda Murrey was a close friend, and her husband, David, an equally good friend of Nigel's. David, an architect, was the type of man who made a party without being the

18

exhibitionist life and soul of it. Freda, blonde hair taken up off her face, had an enormous zest for living and was elegant without any fashion-plate hardness, and her china blue eyes twinkled in what seemed always to be a sun-tanned face.

'A party,' she said as she walked through the door, 'and no excuses.' Her voice was slightly husky and while she spoke quickly, every word was audible.' Tonight.'

They went into the sitting room which Mrs Pringle had quickly left to make coffee. Freda's gaze met Carolyn's as they sat down by the fire. 'You're not too good,' Freda exclaimed with concern. 'Or is it worry?'

Carolyn laughed. 'Neither. A bad mood.'

'Hardly any sleep, I guess. The Martin baby. I'm so glad for Nigel.' The chuckle that followed was eloquent. 'All in one breath, David would say... Now about tonight...'

Carolyn shook her head. 'Impossible, Freda. Hospital day, and a committee meeting afterwards.'

'Damn! It's the Young's. A spur of the moment affair. They asked me to rope you and Nigel in. You know what fun they are.'

Carolyn knew; they were patients as well as friends and kept open house which was always full of laughter and, just then, she needed laughter, almost as a plant needed water.

'Couldn't you come later, or even leave

Nigel to take care of himself while you play truant for the evening?'

Carolyn glanced at the telephone.

Freda sighed. 'I know.' She added, 'Carolyn, I hate friends who butt in, but you hardly get out at all – apart from a dash into Lewes when Mrs Clark is here to take the calls. In the summer it is different, you can enjoy the garden, but the winter... Having friends here, as you do, isn't the same. David and I were talking about it the other night. Oh, yes,' she admitted honestly, 'we both know you don't mind this life, and that you and Nigel are two happy people, but... Ah, well, I shouldn't have...'

'You can say anything you like,' Carolyn interrupted. 'It is true, anyway.'

'I'd call a doctor's life a dog's life in these days,' Freda burst out explosively. 'And as for his wife...'

They laughed together to break the mounting tension. But Freda was not deceived. Carolyn looked unhappy and her laughter was forced; yet, she argued to herself, it was not possible for there suddenly to be something wrong with the marriage.

'Nigel appreciates that angle,' Carolyn put in swiftly and despised her own mood anew, '"I just can't go on like this"' re-echoing and bringing back the sick apprehension. The telephone rang again. Freda groaned. Carolyn reached for her memo pad as she lifted the receiver. Another note was made; another visit for the following day promised. Carolyn knew the case. 'Gall bladder trouble,' she said, as she turned back to Freda. 'My guess is an operation.'

'Having been a nurse must be of enormous value.' Freda spoke admiringly. 'To say nothing of what a help you are to Nigel. You always manage to sound as though you cared about the patient too. Amazing.'

'I hate curt telephone voices,' Carolyn said with feeling. 'That "drop dead" intonation makes me furious.'

'Do you know a doctor named Faber – Max Faber?'

Carolyn shook her head. 'Why?'

'We met him at The Star at Alfriston last night. He's staying there apparently. Attractive. It was talking about voices that brought him to mind.' Freda's eyes twinkled. 'It's one of these come-to-bed voices.'

Carolyn laughed without effort as she suggested, 'Fatal for a doctor!'

'He could have a pretty devastating effect, anyway. He talked as though he might be coming to live in the district. Goody! I warned David. He liked him too, though. You're bound to meet him. I must say he was a big cagey about his plans. Of course I do ask a heap of questions – not curiosity, but interest.'

'David will have to put you on a lead if this

man comes here.'

Freda grinned. 'I must admit that I like attractive men. Just because one is married doesn't mean one lives in blinkers. And a little bit of excitement adds zest. He isn't exactly the flattering type, but he makes you feel important – and a woman.' She nodded her head as she spoke and oozed satisfaction. Carolyn loved her endearing frankness and knew exactly what she meant. Her words struck home.

'Does David make you feel like that?'

'Oh, yes.' Freda's voice lilted. 'I'd hate a man who looked at me as though I were part of the furniture – or looked at me without seeing me, if that doesn't sound too stupid.'

Carolyn felt a tug at her heart which seemed to hurt. 'It doesn't sound stupid at all. I believe that men invite infidelity far more by neglect, or disinterest, than by their other defects.'

Freda was not deaf to the note of seriousness behind the apparently casual utterance. She sighed and changed the subject by saying, 'So I can't persuade you to leave that devil-for-work husband of yours to fend for himself tonight? No, that was just a joke. Poor Nigel is certainly dedicated to his job. I can't think what we should do without him.'

'Send for Doctor Faber,' Carolyn flashed back.

'Dicey,' came the swift retort. 'Nigel's so comfortable somehow.'

'Don't make him sound like a cushion.'

Freda's smile illuminated her face.

'What I say is true, Caro.' The abbreviation of the name was used rarely, but never without significance. 'Nigel makes his patients feel safe, but that doesn't mean it detracts from his charm as a man. When you are ill you never lose sight of him as the doctor ... difficult to explain and you wouldn't know; you're not lucky enough to be his patient!' She glanced at the clock as she spoke. 'The time! I've to be at the hairdresser's in ten minutes.'

Carolyn told the story of the patient Nigel had suffered that morning.

'She's right,' Freda agreed. 'My hair drives me mad. Always greasy.'

'And always looks perfect.'

'Huh, not to me. Now yours – naturally wavy. I know, you'd prefer it straight. Oh, I do wish you and Nigel could come with us tonight. It's never the same without you.'

Carolyn felt suddenly lonely; a desperate loneliness unlike anything she had ever known before. Freda's gaze met hers. There was understanding in her silence which she broke after a few seconds, saying, 'Come over to tea with me on Thursday, and I'll give you all the news.'

'Very well, that would be lovely, Freda. I'll

leave as soon as Mrs Clark arrives. Nigel's tea is no problem because he's always too busy to stop for it. I wish to heaven people would not have their babies during the winter.'

'The aftermath of spring. And the Easter holiday,' Freda suggested and laughed. 'All the same, it's beastly weather, and even I hate the icy roads, but Nigel's a fine driver.'

'It's the bad drivers that worry me,' Carolyn said with vehemence. 'Maniacs who ought never to have licences.'

Freda put both hands up to her cheeks. 'You sounded just like David, then. He goes berserk when he gets on to that subject.'

'As if I didn't know,' Carolyn said smilingly. 'We both go to town on that one and thoroughly enjoy ourselves... David's a darling.'

Freda looked lovingly proud. 'He is, really. Such fun. I couldn't live without laughter.'

Carolyn watched the car as it finally went at full speed down the drive. Her affection for Freda was deep. It was a friendship built on sincerity and understanding, and in that second it seemed like a lamp glowing in the darkness. Tea on Thursday. That would be an outing at least.

Mrs Pringle appeared with a neatly written-out list of things needed from the grocer's; cleaning materials taking priority which made Carolyn smile to herself. Mrs

Pringle was not exactly extravagant, but she always made certain that the cupboards were well filled.

'And we do need more tea towels,' she prompted.

Carolyn at that moment could not have cared less about tea towels, but she said as brightly as possible, 'I'll get some when I go into Lewes, although I must have a stock of them somewhere.'

'The linen cupboard needs clearing out,' Mrs Pringle suggested, believing that it would do Mrs Blake good to have a task which might take her mind off whatever was worrying her. She knew that expression which, although it was calculated to deceive, entirely failed to do so where she, herself, was concerned.

'I'll do it this morning,' Carolyn said, glad of any task which dulled her chaotic thoughts and plunged her into a state bordering on limbo.

When Mrs Clark arrived at two o'clock, Carolyn felt relieved to see her. Mrs Clark was efficient and businesslike; the mother of two daughters and the wife of a teacher at a local school. She had done part-time work ever since her marriage seven years ago. Her mother took charge of the children during her absence in the afternoons, and the extra money Mrs Clark earned enabled the family to have the comforts which, otherwise, would have been denied. She was always cheerful and the patients liked her.

'Hospital days,' she said almost as a form of greeting, 'are always hectic for doctor, and long days for you.'

'What about your long days?' Carolyn asked.

'I love every moment of them and teachers do get good holidays, even though they work far more during that time than the public realise. Jimmy would hate it otherwise.' Her smile was warm, and her eyes bright with happiness. She had an outdoor complexion, with rosy cheeks and a brown skin. 'We both love gardening and that is a good hobby.' It was the first time she had volunteered information about herself. Carolyn could visualise the set-up, and it struck her that it was about time she and Nigel thought in terms of children. A hobby. She supposed children could be that, as well as a vital link in marriage. When she dwelt on the possibility she realised how little Nigel and she had discussed these important factors. Before they were married, three years ago (she being twenty-two and Nigel thirty), they had taken for granted having a family after about two years' freedom together. Now, she asked herself, just what did they discuss? The patients, the Health Service – never themselves, or their emotions. In many respects they might have been brother and sister. The sexual side of their relationship was normal but, recently, unexciting. It was useless trying to escape from this truth despite her reluctance to acknowledge it. Mrs Clark's contented, happy face made her almost envious. Carolyn wanted to continue talking to her, but knew the value of every moment because time was short.

'I mustn't keep you from that typewriter,' she said with a smile. 'Doctor has left all his instructions as usual.'

Mrs Clark had walked into the consulting room, her observant eye taking in every detail. 'The X-rays from Doctor Sims – they don't seem to be here, or...'

Carolyn cried, 'I forgot to ring to remind him.'

'I'll get through now.'

'I could go over and collect them, if necessary.'

Mrs Clark nodded. She picked up the receiver and dialled.

'Out,' she exclaimed briefly after saying a few words to Doctor Sims' secretary. She cupped her hand over the microphone. 'If you could collect them – they are ready.'

Carolyn nodded.

The receiver replaced, Mrs Clark said, 'Wrap up; it's bitterly cold out and even in the car... I was frozen. No heater, admittedly.'

'I'll survive,' Carolyn promised, grateful

for the opportunity of getting out. 'My little Mini car is very warm, and two miles to Piddinghoe won't freeze me. Better have the patient's name,' she added swiftly.

'Mrs Meredith.' The name was uttered with unconscious solemnity.

Carolyn knew the case, because of the many telephone conversations she had taken. 'I'll pray they are negative.'

Carolyn reached Piddinghoe a quarter of an hour later. In the afternoon light, the thatched cottages clustering around the little church of St John glowed with curious luminosity as though golden limes were trained on them and the church itself – standing on a small hill, with its round tower, built of flint in the early English and Norman styles – stood out in sharp relief, creating a scene of infinite peace. Carolyn loved the silence to which one could almost listen and believe that, in it, all the history and the sounds of the past were embodied. For those moments she felt in tune with her surroundings. The wind was rustling through the bare, stark trees. Firs creaked and swayed like massive fans painted on the blue and grey sky. A little of the magic of winter brushed off on her for, despite its disadvantages, Carolyn loved winter, with its fires and lamp light. She hated it only on Nigel's account, but felt an almost sensuous appreciation of sunsets that flamed against a darkening sky.

Dr Sims had returned by the time she reached his house – a half-timbered cottage-type building, with a flagged path leading to a heavy oak door. His housekeeper admitted her just as Doctor Sims crossed the hall.

'Ah, Mrs Blake. I'm just going to snatch a cup of tea; will you join me?'

'I'd love to.' Carolyn liked Donald Sims. He was large, jovial and a fine radiologist. Even though she met him very rarely – mostly at local parties – there was no element of strangeness in his attitude; equally, although he was a man of forty-odd, he never adopted the attitude that he was God's gift to women and that his age lent enchantment to the romantics.

They settled in armchairs drawn up to a welcoming fire. The room had a mellowness about it, despite its elegance. The elegance stamped by his wife who died in child-birth six years previously and, with her, the son who lived only a matter of hours. It was a tragedy that stunned the neighbourhood. Carolyn glanced at her photograph remembering her unusual name, Tresina. A miniature stood on a table close to Donald's chair. The face was reminiscent of Perroneau's painting of the Girl with a Cat. The wide, gentle eyes and serenity of expression which held faint surprise.

Carolyn poured out the tea from a

Georgian pot which she had previously admired. As, standing beside her, he took the cup, she smiled and said with a naturalness he particularly liked, 'This is a lovely break.'

'Lovely to play truant, too. I ought not to be here,' he told her with a confident grin. 'I've an appointment any minute now and my secretary will be champing because I have not done all the reports. By the way, I'm glad to hear that Nigel is thinking of taking a partner, or an assistant. He's a damn good doctor and will go far, but not if he drives himself too hard and too soon.'

Carolyn heard the words with disbelief. But she knew that Donald Sims would not speak lightly. A wave of sickness went over her. '"A partner or an assistant."' And Nigel had not even mentioned, or hinted, at the possibility.

2

Carolyn greeted Nigel that night in a mood of outraged rebellion. His meal was ready and she placed it on the table in the dining-room without looking at, or speaking, to him. He was far too engrossed in his own thoughts to notice the omission, and began to eat automatically. Suddenly – rather like someone surfacing from deep water – he said, noticing her absence from the table, 'Where's yours?'

'I've already eaten,' she replied quietly.

'Oh. I was dog tired by the time the meeting started. All right while you're working, but it hits you when you leave off. Thank heaven it's only nine o'clock and, with luck, we can have an early night. Mrs Martin's fine. I looked in on my way back.' He shook his head as Carolyn offered him some cheese. 'Just coffee.'

'I'll bring it in the other room.'

'Fine.'

Carolyn was trembling as she went into the kitchen. For once she was not prepared to consider how tired he was. Resentment built up until she wished she could fly into a temper or rave, or both. She made the coffee and took it to him, setting the cup down on the table near his chair. He was avidly reading the evening paper and made a sound which could be taken as 'Thank you.' She sat down opposite him. The room was silent, apart from the crackling of the logs. Outside a gale was getting up and rain began to lash the windows. The tension within her mounted until at last she said in a voice so unlike her own that he almost dropped the paper on the floor, 'I understand from Doctor Sims you are thinking of taking a partner, or assistant.'

He looked awkward.

'Yes.'

'Without even saying a word to me.' She stared him out and there was no warmth in her eyes.

Nigel sipped his coffee and said, 'I intended doing so tonight.' He began to be roused. 'I told you last evening that I couldn't go on like this.'

'I told you exactly the same.'

'And just what was that supposed to mean?'

'A general dissatisfaction, call it a sense of frustration, if you like. I didn't marry just to be a cook-housekeeper and telephone minder.'

He looked at her, puckering his brows. Shocked.

'Do you realise what you are saying?'

'I realise perfectly. And I mean every word. To it I can now add that I'm not even in your confidence, so that makes me less of a wife than ever.'

Nigel got up and poured himself a small whisky. 'This is ridiculous.'

'Only because you say so.'

'And you don't think I need any help in the practice?'

Carolyn sighed. To try to make a man understand any emotional problem was like trying to catch a salmon with a match.

'Certainly I think you need it...'

He put in swiftly, 'Then what's all the fuss about? Isn't this rather petty?'

'If it is, then everything connected with our relationship is petty.' She tried to sound calm, but her heart was pounding and she kept her hands tightly clasped so that he should not see how they were trembling. Words had an unhappy knack of conflicting with the essence of the thought behind them. 'I was not concerned with the idea of a possible partnership, but with the fact that you hadn't mentioned the idea to me. It must have been in your mind for some time.' She was studying him intently as she spoke, knowing every shade of his expression and wishing she was incapable of interpreting it.

'That's true,' he admitted. 'I wasn't sure how you would take it.'

She looked at him aghast. 'Have I ever been unsympathetic towards anything you wanted to do?'

'No; but this is different.' He lowered his gaze.

Carolyn jumped to a conclusion as she exclaimed, 'Because the prospective partner, or assistant, happens to be a woman? Is that it?' She tried to sound matter of fact.

'Good lord, no! Heaven forbid! I see enough women.'

Her voice was suddenly firm, 'Look here, Nigel, stop behaving like an adolescent. So you want a partner – an excellent thing, but what is there about it to necessitate my being kept in the dark? Perhaps re-phrasing my question may enable you to give me a direct answer.'

Nigel could not have said just why he was so reluctant to explain the situation. He knew he needed a partner, but he did not *want* one. Mentioning it at all made him feel committed.

'When did you see Dr Sims?'

'This afternoon. I had a cup of tea with him. I went to collect those X-rays.'

'Oh.' His sigh was half weary and half resigned. 'The truth is that if I take the particular partner I have in mind, it would mean his living here until he can find a suitable house.'

'Has all this been done by letter, or have

you met the man?' Carolyn fought against the temptation to explode, knowing that to do so would not serve any good purpose.

'I've met him.'

'I see.' Carolyn had visions of another person sharing the home which she and Nigel had created, and she could not overcome her distaste at the prospect.

'I was going to ask you tonight if he might come for the weekend, so that we could talk things over.' He added rather belligerently, 'I know you're pretty fed up with our life as it is at the moment.'

'I'm more fed up with being shut out of your confidence. That's beyond me. As for asking me if he could come for the weekend ... since when have you needed to *ask* – as though you were some lodger here. The whole thing's fantastic. And I resent it,' she finished on a note of annoyance.

'And I resent your referring to yourself as a "cook-housekeeper-cum-telephone minder".'

She flashed back, 'Doesn't all this prove my point?'

'No; I should hardly ask my housekeeper if I could have a week-end guest.'

'But the chances are that you might have sufficient interest in her opinions to mention the possibility of a partner, or at least to pave the way for the eventuality. Evidently a wife doesn't qualify for the privilege.'

Silence fell between them – an uneasy silence – which made them both unhappy. He broke it by saying, rather curtly, 'And now suppose you tell me what you really meant last night when you said "that makes two of us".'

Carolyn had an uncanny feeling that she was talking to a stranger. Emotion died in that moment as she said, her thoughts crystallising as she spoke, 'I meant that I want to take an active part in the practice, and have more help in the house. I can type and do shorthand. My nursing experience should be of use – to say nothing of having Midwifery as well as my S.R.N.'

He stared at her for a second before rapping out, 'I am aware of your qualifications.'

'There's a wide gulf between awareness and appreciation.'

'I've always appreciated all you can do.' His brows puckered. 'I've never known you in this mood.'

'Circumstances dictate one's mood. I might not have existed, so far as you are concerned, and it's time I did something more stimulating than answering the telephone and taking a few messages.' She hastened on, 'I know how busy you are and how tired you are on most occasions. I don't expect gaiety, or rushing around to parties – you'd hate both, anyway. All I ask is work that enables me to feel alive – someone living instead of merely waiting. You'll need a secretary – a full-time one – when you get a partner. I'm applying for the job.'

The telephone rang to Nigel's accompaniment of 'Damn!'

'Yes, Mrs Philips.' He spoke quietly, but was instantly alert, his expression solemn, even anxious. 'When?'

Mrs Philips... Carolyn knew her. She was a frail brave woman whose husband was an alcoholic.

The receiver went down and Nigel jumped to his feet. 'I must get over there at once. That devil has slashed her arm and tried to suffocate her.'

'Why on earth does she stay with him?'

For a second Nigel paused on his way to the door, his eyes gleamed and his voice held cynicism. 'Possibly because she happens to be in love with him. I've great respect for Mrs Philips.' He had reached the hall by the time he added, 'Don't wait up. I shall have this fellow put into hospital. She's reached breaking point.'

Carolyn said quietly, 'I shall wait up. You'll be glad of some coffee.'

He made no comment until he had hastily put on his overcoat.

'You talked in terms of working in the practice.' His voice was quiet and matter of fact. 'I think it's a good idea, and if you'd like to start now, I'd be grateful if you'd help me out with Mrs Philips.'

Carolyn did not hesitate. She grabbed a coat from a peg in the cloakroom and went out with him into the stormy night. There was tumult within her, because the whole conversation had been off key and she felt – despite justification – that she had put her case badly. Neither really understood the other's point of view, and they seemed to have lost all hope of communication.

Nigel drove as fast as was possible along the road on the east side of the Ouse, passing near the foot of Beddingham Hill and joining the Lewes-Polgate road at Beddingham, finally reaching the suburb of the Cliffe where the Philips' had a half-timbered cottage-type house, which Mrs Philips owned and maintained from money left to her by her father. Lights were at every window and the front door opened before Nigel and Carolyn had begun to walk down the short crazy-paved pathway.

'This,' Nigel murmured, 'won't be a pleasant sight.'

'Nurses are not trained to see pleasant sights,' she replied.

Mrs Philips greeted them breathlessly. 'Thank God you're here, Doctor.'

Nigel looked at her bruised face and blackened eye, his gaze dropping to the crude, blood-soaked rag around her right arm. Shouting and banging came from a room nearby.

'I managed to get out and lock the door,' she explained. 'He'd smashed a glass – that's how I got this.' She indicated the bandage which fell away, revealing a nasty gash. 'He threw me on to the sofa and held a cushion over my face.' She finished desperately, 'I can't stand any more; I just can't *stand* any more.' There was a note of helpless apology in her trembling voice.

'You won't have to,' Nigel said grimly. 'My wife will look after you for the moment. I'll attend to him.'

Mrs Philips handed over the key which was clutched tightly in her left hand.

Carolyn slipped back into the world of nursing after a second of sickening apprehension. Nigel gave her his bag and she helped Mrs Philips up the stairs to a twin-bedded room, settling her back against the pillows and placing the eiderdown over her trembling body. The bathroom was adjoining. 'Just lie quietly,' she murmured softly. 'I was a nurse before I married, and we'll have you more comfortable as quickly as we can.'

Mrs Philips' eyes filled with tears, but she was too weak, too desperate, really to cry. 'I feel so ashamed,' she whispered. 'So *ashamed*.'

'You are very brave,' Carolyn said with feeling, assessing the depth of the wound in the arm and realising that stitches would be needed. Swiftly, having found everything necessary for her use, she attended to the bruised, torn flesh, carefully removing the tiny splinters of glass. That done, she went downstairs and filled a bowl with ice cubes from the refrigerator. The black eye needed an ice pack to reduce the swelling and this she administered. The shouting from the room below continued, but less stridently. Then it ceased, and Mrs Philips stirred, her fear pathetic. 'I don't want to see him,' she cried. 'Please tell Doctor.'

Carolyn soothed her. The house was filled with an atmosphere of violence and degradation, as though it had taken to itself some of the horror of that, and many other, nights.

Nigel came into the bedroom. Carolyn had put everything out for his use and he glanced at her approvingly as he swiftly gave a local anaesthetic before suturing the wounded arm. Mrs Philips hardly stirred; she had reached a point where exhaustion deadened both mental and physical suffering.

Nigel felt great compassion for Glenda Philips. She had been his patient for several years and had fought the deadly scourge of alcohol almost from the day she married. Her love, her courage, her superhuman faith, had sustained her; but now, he knew, her spirit was broken and only a harsh reality was left in the bleakness of failure.

She had fought to save her marriage; sacrificed her desire for a family, and been prepared to endanger her own life rather than admit defeat in what had always been a losing battle. Knowing her as he did, he said without prevarication, 'I'm having your husband sent to hospital. The ambulance is on its way. Only people trained in the treatment of this disease can be of the slightest use to him.'

Mrs Philips' mouth puckered. In that second, it was not the vicious alcoholic she remembered, but the man with whom she had fallen so desperately in love when she was twenty; the man who had cunningly and skilfully kept his grim secret from her. She betrayed, by a gesture, both her distaste and her assent. Her heart seemed like a great well of misery and loneliness.

'And when I've examined you,' Nigel went on, 'I'm having you taken to hospital for a complete rest. There's no argument. I've made the arrangements.' To his astonishment and relief, no protest was forthcoming, but in that second a spasm of pain shook her and she turned, instinctively, to Carolyn. 'Could you help me? Something is wrong. I was terrified I might be pregnant and now...' Her voice dropped; she caught her breath as the pain increased, managing to add, 'You'll find towels – everything in the linen cupboard over there.'

Nigel and Carolyn exchanged glances and both knew that they now had a miscarriage on their hands. As Carolyn took towels and linen from the cupboard, the sound of an ambulance drawing up outside the house broke the almost uncanny silence.

'He doesn't know anything about all this,' Mrs Philips said pitifully. Then, 'He'll be looked after properly, won't he? He's kind when he's sober.'

'They will do everything in their power,' Nigel promised. 'He won't know anything about the journey; he's in far too deep a stupor.'

She nodded and Nigel went downstairs, leaving Carolyn to take over. When he had mentioned the examination, he had thought in terms of making certain that she had not suffered any more damage than the visible signs betrayed. The possibility of a pregnancy had not occurred to him.

When he returned to the bedroom, Mrs Philips was all prepared and thankful for Carolyn's gentleness and sympathy as she had undressed her and done everything to make her more comfortable.

'Now,' Nigel said reassuringly, as he began his examination. He had already telephoned the hospital again and an ambulance was being sent. It was, he thought, one of those blessings that he had previously arranged for her to be admitted. In these circumstances there would be no delay. He knew that there was no question of this case representing any false alarm in which rest might allow the pregnancy to go to term. The haemorrhage was too severe and the manner in which it had been brought on could mean only a complete abortion.

A little later, wrapped in blankets, she was taken on a stretcher to the ambulance. Both Nigel and Carolyn accompanied her. It was now very late; the roads were deserted and it seemed a matter of minutes before they reached the hospital, which loomed as a sanctuary set against the dark canopy of the sky.

Night Sister came towards Nigel and Carolyn as the stretcher was placed on a trolley. Nigel had already given her all the particulars and she looked down at Mrs Philips as to say, 'Don't worry; we're here to take care of you.' Her voice in greeting was soft and kind. She was greatly beloved among both patients and staff.

Mrs Philips held out her left hand to Carolyn. 'So good to me,' she whispered... 'Thank you, Doctor.'

'I'll be in to see you tomorrow,' Nigel promised. 'And keep you informed.'

The trolley moved swiftly and surely towards the lifts. Another patient; another life story to add to the hundreds, even thousands, written in silence behind the sheltering hospital walls.

'And she is such a sweet person,' Carolyn said with emotion. 'To suffer all this through that – that *creature*.'

'She,' Nigel commented, 'will recover; he never will. He's too far gone. Unfortunately people like him have nine lives... And we haven't a car,' he added swiftly. 'I'll have to get on to the garage; at least their hire service will still be operating, thank heaven.'

They reached home just before midnight. Few words had been spoken during the drive back, but when they had removed their coats and Nigel had poured himself out a whisky, he said, 'That was one way to get your hand in again. You did well, Carolyn.'

Carolyn! The name sounded so aloof, so strange, to her.

'Thank you. I'm grateful I was there.' She broke off, then hastened, 'She's so thin. I didn't realise how thin until I undressed her. It was like tending a child, somehow.'

Nigel made a sound that was half fury, half compassion. 'A child,' he echoed, 'and how she would have loved one.'

'There's no hope this time, is there?'

He looked grave. 'I think they'll operate and she'll probably need a transfusion. The haemorrhage was too heavy.'

Carolyn felt that she was standing on an island, emotionally dead. It was too late, and they were both too tired, to discuss their own problems, or make any plans. They went up to bed in silence, but just before turning off the light, Carolyn asked, 'By the way, who is this prospective partner and week-end guest. What is his name?'

'Max Faber.'

'Staying at The Star,' Carolyn said coolly.

Nigel's voice was suddenly alert. 'How did you know?'

'Freda happened to mention him. She and David had been over to Alfriston.' As she spoke she slipped into bed, keeping to the edge of it. 'Africa is not the only place where they have tom toms.'

3

It was after surgery the following evening that Nigel said, as he drew his chair closer to the fire and relaxed for the first time since early morning, 'I think it would be a good idea if you telephoned Doctor Faber and invited him over this week-end.'

Carolyn tried not to build up her natural resistance. Obviously Nigel had no intention of discussing their own problems further and had taken her strictly at her word regarding the practice and her future work in it. She could not gauge either his pleasure or displeasure at the prospect. She longed to explain her feelings, but his expression was inscrutable and destroyed her confidence.

'Very well,' she agreed. 'I assume you have already mentioned the possibility, so that I shall not be springing any surprise.' She succeeded in keeping her voice calm and matter of fact.

'I did not go into detail. Of course, seeing that Alfriston is so near, he could come over for the day on Sunday.' He lit a cigarette. 'But I always think you can tell more about a person if you have him, or her, under your roof for two or three days, than you could ever discover by seeing them for a few hours over many years.'

Carolyn said with a touch of unconscious defiance, 'In any case it will be pleasant to have someone to talk to. We might even manage to get out for a meal. I'll try The Star now, if you like.'

'By all means.'

Carolyn tried. Doctor Faber was out. She returned to her chair and silence fell. This was an evening for which she had longed. To have Nigel with her for an hour or two, without interruption, was a major event. Now that he was here with what looked like every prospect of remaining, she found that there was nothing she had to say; nothing that would not lead to an argument.

They had their evening meal and she left the washing up for Mrs Pringle.

'How was Mrs Philips?' she asked as she drank her coffee.

'They operated and had to set up a drip. She'll be all right. He's in pretty bad shape. I can see him ending up in a mental home.'

'Life's crazy,' Carolyn said vehemently.

'People are. Life is what we make it.' Nigel was trying to fathom Carolyn's mood and incapable of assessing it. 'Anything on television?'

'The usual drivel, no doubt. Dustbins and kitchen sinks.' She got up as she spoke and turned the set on. A howling and screeching came at them as the sound blasted before the picture which, when it appeared, was of cedar-mop-haired youths gyrating to a hideous cacophony. Carolyn gave vent to her feelings by giving the switch a vigorous jerk. The screen went dark. 'At least we have the privilege of not being forced to watch,' she exclaimed.

'You could try the other channel.'

Carolyn tried. 'Advertisements. Detergents.' Again the screen went dark. She returned to her chair just as the telephone rang. It was the first time she could ever recall welcoming it at this hour.

'Oh, yes, Mrs Winton. When?'

Carolyn watched Nigel's face cloud in immediate concern. She knew that Mrs Winton was not due for another month and that she had miscarried twice before.

'I'll come immediately.' Then as he replaced the receiver he said, 'Damn! She's losing.' He kicked off his slippers and thrust his feet into his discarded shoes. 'I ought never to take them off,' he added with an attempt at humour.

'Can I help?'

'No; her sister is with her. She's a district nurse, having a few days' holiday.' His brows puckered. 'There's nothing we've overlooked in this case – nothing. She's either been in bed or resting, most of the time.'

Carolyn went into his consulting room as he put on his coat. She swiftly checked his bag and handed it to him. He opened the front door and a flurry of snow blew in. The drive and garden stretched white against the darkness of the sky. Snow and treacherous roads made night calls doubly hazardous. She watched the car carve two furrows that looked like icing sugar. The exhaust gave out its smoke and the rear light shone brightly in the frosty air. As she turned back into the house, the telephone rang and when she answered it a voice said, 'My name is Faber – Doctor Faber – could I speak to Doctor Blake?'

Carolyn introduced herself, and mentioned the invitation which was immediately accepted. She thought of Freda as she sat there talking, finding it easy to converse and to laugh, although Max Faber was a stranger. His voice was attractive and its intonation brought an intimate awareness of him. She felt less lonely and cut off, the prospect of his visit creating a certain excitement for no better reason than that she was unhappy and unsettled, and he provided a diversion. It was agreed that he should arrive for dinner on Friday evening.

As she replaced the receiver it seemed that her world had changed completely. No doubt the man was charming and would make as little nuisance of himself as possible in the house, but that did not alter the fact that her privacy with Nigel would inevitably be affected. On the other hand, she argued to herself, Nigel badly needed help and was grossly overworked. Probably the advent of Max Faber would enable her to have a great deal more of Nigel's company. She could hardly have less than now, she thought bitterly. Yet none of this took away the hurt of Nigel's secrecy, or the fact that he had not given any explanation for his behaviour. She tried to read, to take her mind off the problem, but the words failed to register. Better wash up; the idea was distasteful... Freda would be astonished about Max Faber, when she told her tomorrow. Was tomorrow Thursday? The days had seemed just a muddle since the previous Sunday – probably because she was in emotional chaos.

It was just before eleven that she heard Nigel's car drive into the garage. The snow was thick as she opened the front door, with little drifts already piling up at the corners of the one step leading from the pathway into the porch. The beam of golden light from the hall poured out into the darkness and guided Nigel to the house. He didn't speak until he had removed his coat, but she knew by his expression and the pallor of his face, that something was wrong. He looked at her – staring almost.

'I couldn't save either of them,' he said,

sagging down on to the dark oak settle as though his legs refused to support him any longer. 'I got Ensmore in.' His voice was husky.

Ensmore – Graham Ensmore – was one of the finest gynaecologists in Sussex. Fortunately, Carolyn thought, his home was in Lewes.

'I'm so sorry,' she said shakenly.

He dragged himself to his feet and walked towards his chair in the sitting-room, flopping into it, then stooping to take off his shoes and thrusting his feet into the previously discarded slippers.

Carolyn poured him out a brandy which he took gratefully. In those moments he seemed like a tired middle-aged man and her heart ached for him. She did not question, and he did not volunteer any information. He sat there, staring into the fire and turning his glass in a circular movement – a habit in moments of stress.

Carolyn broke the heavy silence by mentioning Max Faber. 'He's coming over on Friday for dinner.'

Nigel looked at her with half critical inquiry. 'And not for the week-end?'

She replied patiently, 'Of course for the week-end. That was what you wanted, unless I misunderstood you.'

'How did you think he sounded?'

'Charming; attractive voice. I imagine he

51

has a good sense of humour.'

'God help him if he hasn't. In this profession you need to be a laughing hyena ... Eric Winton is almost demented. They'd made so many plans and they were so happy together. I see little of that,' he finished half cynically. 'I'm glad Faber's coming,' he went on disjointedly, and Carolyn felt that she might not have been there. 'All things being equal, he can take over some of the donkey work and let me have five minutes peace.'

Carolyn made allowances for his mood, but even doing so did not render her deaf to the fact that he talked in the singular and that there was no hint that *they* might have a little more time together.

There were no more calls that night and Nigel slept exhausted. Carolyn remained awake, thoughts chasing through her mind in a series of distortions, until she reached a point where she convinced herself that her marriage was a complete failure and Nigel no longer had any love for her – or she for him! When it was time to get up she was ready to sleep, but dragged herself from the bed and went downstairs in a daze, plugging in the electric kettle and lighting the gas! The absurdity restored a little sanity. She drew the curtains and a Christmas card scene met her gaze. The snow was deep and the last pale flush of dawn touched it with a soft pink glow. The by-roads would be treacherous and even as the thought went through her mind, the sound of cars crashing broke the silence. Cracking glass and the impact of metal against metal was all too familiar in the road nearby. Nigel's plate on the wide gate provided obvious guidance for any casualties.

Carolyn hurried to the front door and opened it. People were already running down the road, seeming to have come up from holes in the ground, for the area was sparsely populated. A man came rushing up the drive calling, 'Doctor! Doctor!'

It was not necessary for Carolyn to rouse Nigel. Having heard the crash, he had hastily donned his trousers, keeping on his pyjama jacket, and had reached the hall as though airborne. Carolyn almost threw him his overcoat and thrust his bag into his hand. The man now standing at the door had superficial cuts and bruises, but appeared to be oblivious of them. At the sight of Nigel – whom he knew – he cried, 'A woman is trapped and the man with her... It's terrible. The car came at me... I'm all right – just shaken up!' They were hurrying away as he spoke and Nigel flung words to Carolyn, 'Get on to the police.'

Carolyn knew the routine. She could not leave the house to be of assistance because the telephone must be answered. She made the call to the police and then set up the trolley. One never knew, in these cases, just who might need attention.

Mrs Pringle came in, white-faced and trembling. 'Dreadful,' she murmured, half to herself. 'The blood on the snow and doctor working – kneeling. He'll catch his death this weather. Police there, and the ambulance came up as I passed.'

'I heard,' Carolyn said.

'It's doctor I worry about,' Mrs Pringle went on angrily. These mad things on the road. Wouldn't matter if they just killed themselves – good riddance to them, I say. But oh, no! They ruin other people's lives. And doctor out there, dragged from his bed...!' She managed to pause long enough to draw breath.

Carolyn said reassuringly, 'Doctor will be all right. Just think of all the epidemics he escapes. The cold won't worry him – only the injured.'

'I'll make some porridge,' Mrs Pringle said as though it were a weapon directed at those who disturbed Nigel's peace. 'He'll be needing a good lining in his stomach after all this.'

Carolyn turned away to hide her smile. The word 'lining' made Nigel sound like a garment.

'Doctor would enjoy that, Mrs Pringle,' she said appreciatively. 'Better wait before starting to cook the bacon. One never quite knows how long he may be, but if the ambulance is there...'

Mrs Pringle nodded.

Carolyn wondered just then how the changes about to take place in the household would be received by her. Until all the details had been settled, it was better, wiser, to remain silent.

Nigel returned about ten minutes later and was thankful for the cup of tea which Mrs Pringle gave him.

'Mrs Manners was in that crash.' His voice changed. Mrs Manners was one of his first patients and his diagnosis and tenacity in face of opposition, had spared her the removal of her left breast and had been in the nature of a triumph among his colleagues.

'Oh, no.' Carolyn had a genuine affection for Anne Manners. 'Not – badly–'

'Nothing can save her; broken spine; both lungs pierced.' He finished almost harshly. 'The maniac at the wheel was driving her into Brighton to see her mother who had been rushed to hospital – *he* escaped with minor cuts. Came out of that side turning without looking to right or left, according to the poor devil who came here. If I had my way I'd make every motorist accused of dangerous driving sit in casualty and watch the human wrecks that are brought in. Might give them food for thought. And all this chap could snivel about was that he was helping out because the Manners' car wouldn't start. Alec Manners is in Zürich on business. The two boys are, as you know, at Brighton College. I'll go over there and break the news to them – perhaps they'd prefer it that way. Mrs Manners' sister lives in Scotland. She can't get down quickly. I imagine the planes will be grounded in this weather, anyway.' He added, at war with the world, 'And the trains will certainly be running late.'

Carolyn nodded. She felt the weight of Nigel's depression.

'Could this have been a skid?'

'No.' He glanced at the clock. 'Bah. Surgery will be late.'

'I'll deal with the people,' Carolyn said, 'although, by now, everyone will know what has happened. Births, deaths and accidents are the high-lights of gossip.'

Nigel just looked at her as he began to mount the stairs. His trousers were blood-stained, his hair ruffled. 'Get Mrs Pringle to hurry breakfast... Damn!'

Carolyn answered the telephone. Mrs Clark said, 'I'm so sorry, Mrs Blake, but I'm feeling very ill – really ill. I'm afraid it's flu. I hate to worry Doctor, but if he could call... And there's the work–' Her voice grew fainter.

Carolyn reassured her, promising that she would be visited as soon as possible. 'Flu!'

Heaven spare them an epidemic. As she replaced the receiver, the thought flashed through her mind that this meant cancelling her date with Freda.

Nigel was avidly consuming his porridge when Carolyn mentioned Mrs Clark. He said caustically, 'That leaves you holding the baby – a rather premature baby. Splendid opportunity for you to see how you like sitting at a desk, typing. I'll visit Mrs Clark. These bronchial types can be pretty ill.' He glanced out of the window as he spoke. It had begun to snow again, and the sky looked dark and angry. 'Lewes High Street will be excellent for skating,' Nigel went on facetiously, trying to forget the harrowing scene that was all too familiar, and yet which never failed to upset him. He was eating because he knew that it was unlikely he would have an opportunity of doing so again until the evening.

Carolyn showed no signs of the emotion that was churning within her. She could visualise the steep hill and the skidding cars as they braked. 'You have several appointments here after five,' she reminded him.

'One I dread, the cervical smear was positive.' He added with almost passionate concern, 'and she's young – thirty. Unless I'm mistaken, it means taking away everything.'

'Ovaries?'

He nodded. 'A pretty grim prognosis.'

Carolyn knew that they were both falling back on the one topic of conversation that did not embrace personal emotion. The intimacy between them had died, and in its place had come a rather stilted politeness. Silences became awkward; thoughts dare not be expressed.

'Is there more coffee?'

'Plenty.' She took his cup and re-filled it.

'I'll have to give you all the instructions for today,' he said calmly.

Her voice rose a little. 'Nigel, we must talk – discuss–'

He interrupted, 'You get the additional help you need in the house, then the work in the practice can be sorted out. Mrs Clark will show you the ropes and certainly be snapped up by any of the doctors around here. Nothing to discuss. A fact is a fact.'

It left her no loophole whereby she might discover if he resented the prospective change.

'I'll see how many patients are waiting,' she murmured and went from the room into the surgery which led from Nigel's consulting room and had a separate entrance so that people could admit themselves. The sound of coughing came to her ears before she reached the row of faces, each in their different stages of misery. The genuinely sick, who should not have been out, but who 'didn't want to worry the doctor', the martyrs who moaned that they were crippled with arthritis when, in truth, they had a touch of rheumatism; and the anxious mothers trying to keep their fractious offspring quiet. All these, Carolyn took in at a glance until, finally, her gaze fell on a girl sitting apart from the rest; a girl whose eyes were like a hunted deer and whose condition, while not apparent, Carolyn sensed. Her heart sank. She knew the family well. The father owned a confectioner's shop in Lewes and was a hard-working, respectable citizen whose three children were a credit to him since he was a widower and had brought them up with only the aid of a daily help. Moreen, the youngest – now staring at Carolyn with beseeching eyes – was the only girl, and about seventeen.

Nigel appeared in the doorway. 'First patient,' he said pleasantly.

Moreen Fuller stood up and moved forward, forcing a cough that became a nervous spasm. Once in the consulting room, she said bleakly and as though she could not endure the burden of her own secret any longer, 'I think I'm going to have a baby.'

Nigel was used to pretence, lies, blatant deceit; he was also used to tears, but this bald statement of fact seemed more poignant than any subterfuge. 'Then,' he replied gently, 'we'd better make sure.'

She relaxed slightly. 'I've dreaded telling you. You've always been so good to us all – a friend.'

'A doctor is always a friend if he is allowed to be, and the patient is honest with him.' He smiled encouragingly.

Moreen went into the examining room and undressed, leaving only her slip on. For those few moments she felt secure. The warmth of the couch was soothing and she lay looking at the ceiling as though transported into another world.

Nigel examined her, his questions were asked in a gentle reassuring tone. Not much doubt; the cervix was soft; the breasts tender. About ten weeks.

'I am – it's true, isn't it?' Her large eyes seemed like black grapes in a white face.

'I'm afraid so. Get dressed. I must talk to you. Can you wait until I've seen the other patients.'

'Oh, yes – anything.'

Nigel left her and called for Carolyn. 'Take Moreen into the sitting-room. Give her a cup of tea.'

Carolyn nodded and did as she was asked. Mrs Pringle made some tea and Moreen drank it gratefully, huddled over the fire feeling suddenly icy cold. She looked at Carolyn and whispered, 'You're very kind. I

60

want to be brave. I felt you knew when you saw me in the surgery.'

A pang went through Carolyn's heart. What agony of mind, what nightmares had this child – for she seemed little more – lived through until this moment? She was beautiful, with corn-coloured hair that curled up at shoulder length. Her skin was like alabaster.

'I wondered, but then I'm trained to wonder,' Carolyn hastened.

'Meaning that ordinary people wouldn't know?'

Carolyn nodded comfortingly.

'My father mustn't know.' It was a cry. 'Somehow I must manage.' She rushed on, 'He's been so good – a mother and father, too. Worked so hard to give us all a good education. We've been *friends.*'

'Do you think a friend would like to be shut out of any trouble?'

'This is different.' The silence became ominous. 'I've tried to think of something I could *do–*'

At that moment Nigel appeared in the doorway. Carolyn moved quickly from the room.

'Now,' Nigel said firmly, 'we don't want to hear anything like that. Understand? I want your promise about this, or I cannot take on your case.'

Moreen lowered her head and colour

mounted her cheeks. 'I'm sorry, Doctor, but I've been desperate. What can I do? Where can I go?'

'First of all, does the man know?'

She shook her head. 'He will never know,' she said vehemently.

'Because you do not wish to marry him?' Nigel tried to fathom her attitude.

'He would not marry me. He doesn't love me. It was just one of those things. I can't explain,' she rushed on. 'I didn't seem to have any will power. I love him, you see,' she said simply.

'If this man doesn't know the truth, how can you be so sure he wouldn't marry you?' Nigel was persistent because he knew she was withholding some part of the truth. 'If I saw him–'

Instantly she cried, 'No – no! I don't want that.'

'Because he is already married?'

She lowered her gaze. 'No; engaged. I'm not blaming him and I don't want to cause any trouble.' She added looking at Nigel very levelly. 'There's not been anyone else, Doctor.'

'I believe that, Moreen.'

'I don't want any enquiries made about him. It's all over.' A note of desolation crept into her voice. 'We were together just a fortnight – that's all. You see, the girl he's going to – to marry–' her voice broke, 'she's visit-

ing her parents in America. He's going out
to join her at Christmas.'

There was a pause before Nigel asked,
'Did he tell you about his engagement at the
beginning?'

Faint defiance crept into her eyes. 'We
neither of us told the other anything. He
was honest with me after – afterwards. Trying to blame him won't make my position
any better.'

Nigel was amazed by her maturity and
the lack of self-pity. Usually he was confronted with tears and recriminations. The
blame was seldom shared. He found this
terrified (and he had no doubt she was terrified) acceptance far more difficult to deal
with.

'I'm certainly not a believer in marriage
being the only solution to this kind of
problem,' he said firmly. 'There is no simple
answer. It is a question of doing what is
best.' He glanced at his watch. 'I'd like to
talk to you – I haven't time now. You will
have to decide whether you are going to
leave the district, have the baby adopted, or
keep it.'

'I don't want my father to know,' she said
adamantly. She got to her feet. 'Thank you
for being so kind. I feel better having
talked.'

Nigel could not help saying urgently,
'Moreen, won't you tell me the name of the

man? He might help you – quite apart from the question of–'

She cut in with a fierce determination, 'No. Words can't make any difference. And I shall never tell anyone his name. I'll think over what you've said to me.'

'Come to see me on Monday next. After evening surgery. That will give you time to weigh it all up very carefully.'

She nodded, her gaze seeming faraway. 'At least I'm not sick,' she said thankfully and irrelevantly. 'I couldn't stay at home if I were. As it is, I've been helping my father out in the shop because one of his assistants is away ill. I wanted to be a nurse, but I was too young to begin training.'

'But not to apply,' he suggested, 'or was it all this–'

She interrupted swiftly, 'Yes; I went to London for a holiday–' She broke off and sighed at the recollection of her own excitement when she left home. How different it all was now.

'Did you tell your father you were coming here?'

'Yes; I've been coughing – trying to cough – and said I had a sore throat. He wanted to ask you to call, but I managed to persuade him it wasn't bad enough for that... If you could give me a prescription for just *something.*'

Nigel went to his consulting room and

returned, saying, 'Get this made up. It is a gargle.'

She took the prescription and her eyes were full of the gratitude she could not express.

Outside the snow was piling up, and the wind was blowing it in a swirling mass, blanketing the windows as it froze on them.

'I'll give you a lift back to Lewes,' Nigel said swiftly. 'I have several patients to see there and it will save you waiting about for a bus.' He went to the door and called to Carolyn, who quickly came from the kitchen. 'Ask Mrs Pringle to make some tea,' he said hurriedly, 'and then we'll go through the work that must be done today.' He glanced back at Moreen. 'Make yourself comfortable. I shall not be ready for at least half-an-hour.'

Carolyn faced him, a few minutes later, in the consulting room. 'Now,' he began in a matter-of-fact voice. His gaze caught sight of the letters, opened, and piled neatly on his desk.

'If you will dictate the answers,' Carolyn suggested, 'I can have them ready for your signature when you get back. My shorthand is bound to be rusty, but I can improvise.' She picked up her note pad and pencil, sat down in a chair at the other side of his desk, and waited. A cold detachment wiped out emotion.

Nigel dictated six letters. 'I haven't time for this report,' he said, putting aside various notes and a long epistle accompanying them. 'You'd better go through the case sheets and familiarise yourself with the names and all the rest of it. You know the file.'

Carolyn said calmly, and with a trace of cynicism which escaped him, 'Yes, I know the file.' She added, 'And I'll have a boil up so that everything is in order by five o'clock.' She indicated the steriliser as she spoke.

'At least I shall not have to teach you the names of the instruments... I must drop those smears in to the hospital.' He glanced at the slides needing a path report.

'And I'll study the appointments book so that I do not duplicate any sessions that Mrs Clark arranged.'

'Good.' The wind increased in force. 'Why on earth I chose to have a country practice, God knows!'

'Possibly because you preferred the country and this practice was available.' Actually they had both wanted to be in the country and the desire had added to the harmony between them. Carolyn tried not to remember the happiness they had shared in those days.

He avoided her gaze and exclaimed half humorously, 'And I hope I may have one day without miscarriages, and that I'm well out of range of any more accidents!'

Carolyn forced a smile. 'Would you like a coffee before you leave?'

'No time, now. I didn't reckon on having Moreen to deal with. *She* won't miscarry,' he added bitterly.

Carolyn felt that she must strike a note of intimacy; it did not matter who was right, or wrong.

'Nigel,' she began breathlessly, 'could we–'

He was moving towards the door and said, as though she had not begun to speak, 'A Mrs Barker will ring this afternoon. New patient. Lives at Fulmer. Ensmore wants me to take her on, so fit her in as best you can.' With that he went out into the hall and into the sitting room, calling to Moreen, 'Ready?'

Carolyn saw them to the door. The snow blew in the moment she opened it. The garden, apart from the trees, was obliterated. The short drive had merged with the grass verges.

'Don't stand there,' Nigel said swiftly. 'Can't afford another patient now.'

Carolyn managed to smile at Moreen before shutting the door.

Mrs Pringle, crossing the hall at that moment, could not help seeing that tears filled Carolyn's eyes. Agitation mingled with her own distress, but she discreetly turned into the dining room. To her, the house suddenly lay in shadow. Laughter had gone from it.

4

Max Faber arrived punctually at seven o'clock on Friday evening as arranged. Snow had packed itself on the roads and frost had hardened it dangerously. The few miles from Alfriston seemed as hazardous as mountaineering. To make matters worse, he had forgotten the name of the Blake house and had to ask at a cottage if they could help him. A small girl of about eight beamed at him and said proudly, 'That's our doctor. His house is called Downs Cottage.' She gave a little giggle. 'It's a funny name because it isn't a cottage at all; it's a huge house.' She emphasised the last two words and added, 'You can see the lights from it from here – through the trees.' By this time both father and mother had appeared and added their comments, the father finishing with, 'If you keep straight on and then turn first left, it's the only house on the right in that road.'

Max Faber reached Downs Cottage in a matter of five minutes.

Carolyn greeted him not knowing quite what she expected to see, but Freda was not a bad judge of men, and Carolyn felt that there would be truth in her description – which there was. Max Faber was attractive, and with a dominant personality; his voice added to his obvious charm.

'The roads are foul,' he admitted, 'and seeing that I have a memory like a sieve, I forgot the name of your house!'

Carolyn smiled at him rather whimsically. 'Doctors need good memories,' she said, 'but seldom have them. I'm quite convinced that, but for their wives, or secretaries, half the population would be dead!'

'Not a bad idea at that!' The warmth of the house came at him in an almost sensuous wave and, with it, the pleasant homely smell of good cooking.

'But hardly profitable,' she flashed back, aware that she was laughing for the first time for days. She led the way into the sitting room, and after having poured their drinks, settled in a chair immediately opposite his, and explained, 'I'm afraid my husband was called out. Diabetic coma. We've had everything this week.' She was conscious of Max Faber's gaze steadily upon her – a gaze of assessment.

'The "we" meaning that you work in the practice?'

'I have just started to do so,' Carolyn said quietly. 'Before I was just the doctor's wife answering the telephone when there was no one else to do so, or taking messages for the same reason. Neither profit nor satisfaction in it.' She laughed. 'That's harshly put, but having been a nurse before I married, I suppose the bug is still there and, since I can type and do shorthand, it seems foolish to waste my time at the sink.'

He was still studying her. 'And you are not in love with sinks?'

She made a wry face. 'Not unless the need for me to be is really urgent. If you and my husband agree to work together, I shall get someone to take over my sink job.'

Carolyn was hearing herself laugh and talk, feeling rather like an over-wound clock beginning to unwind.

'Then it becomes a vital necessity for me to join forces,' he commented swiftly and with a broad smile.

What type of man was he? Carolyn asked herself, liking his direct gaze and clear grey eyes. His hair was dark brown and his features rugged. A kind man, she decided. Probably calculating where his own assets were concerned.

'And what is your verdict?' The question was disconcerting. 'I'm not a bad thought reader,' he added. 'I'd like your summing up.'

'I never sum people up in a matter of minutes,' she answered quietly.

He still held her gaze. 'Fair enough. I wondered if you might resent my being included in the household – at least until I can get a flat, or house, or whatever is available.'

Carolyn admitted honestly, 'I should not like the arrangement permanently, but I shall be thankful for my husband to have someone with whom to share the work.' She paused. 'I can hear his car now.'

'You have very acute hearing.'

'So would you, were you the wife of a doctor,' she retorted with a laugh.

'I know; we're always late.'

Nigel came in, greeting Max Faber with warmth, but not effusiveness. He refilled the empty glasses and poured himself out a drink. 'The roads are becoming impassable,' he said as he sat down thankfully in his chair. His gaze turned upon Carolyn for a second and moved away swiftly. Her eyes were bright and her expression happier than he had seen it for some time. The light fell on her chestnut hair catching at the sorrel tints which blended with the gold thread in her simple brocade dress – a dress which emphasised her slender figure. Obviously, he thought with relief, Faber had made a good impression. Carolyn could be very withdrawn and cool towards those whom she did not like.

After serving an excellent meal, she left the two men alone together. From the tone of the conversation, it was obvious that much had already been thrashed out between them, and she tried to curb the resentment that crept back as she dwelt once more on Nigel's secrecy. It had never been their policy to allow any differences between them to slide into silence, and while she was thankful that Max Faber appeared to be an extremely pleasant and amusing person, nevertheless he represented, to her, evidence of the gulf that had made Nigel seem almost a stranger with whom it was impossible to communicate. When she re-joined them it was to hear Nigel say, 'Doctor Faber is going to help me out at once. I think we've covered all the ground for the moment. The thing is for him to see the possible accommodation here. You and I have not discussed that.'

Carolyn felt bristly. 'Not discussed that', when he flatly refused to talk. She said with a touch of cynicism, 'I hardly think the word "discuss" comes into it... Anyway, suppose we go over the house? At the moment, only one bedroom is occupied and there are five.' As she spoke she felt that at *any* moment she would move into a room of her own.

The three of them went upstairs. Carolyn said as they reached the landing, 'There is a second staircase, Doctor Faber, which almost makes what was once a study and this bedroom–' she opened the door as she spoke – 'self contained.'

Nigel explained, 'This part of the place is nearly an ancient dwelling. The rest of it, of course, has been modernised and built on to.'

'But this is a marvellous room,' Max Faber said with enthusiasm. 'I like the beams and the chintz, to say nothing of that four poster! Not the thing for any doctor on night call.' He laughed, 'And I have not overlooked our arch enemy, the telephone!'

'The view of the Downs compensates,' Carolyn promised. 'Oh, there is a bathroom and lavatory immediately opposite. All this was done by the previous owners when their family increased. We slept in this room when we first moved in, otherwise it is used only when we have guests. I snatch a bath here when there's no hope of using the one adjoining our room.'

'Since when,' Nigel asked, 'have you not been able to use ours?'

'When you are late.'

'Simple; you be early.'

'I always am.'

Max Faber decided that he could not make up his mind about these two. The last thing he wanted was to be drawn into any marriage problem, but he did not dwell on the matter as he looked down the long wide corridor ahead. It was close carpeted in a shade of deep rose. Everything about the house appealed to him.

'We're tucked away round the corner on the left,' Carolyn went on. 'At first I thought I was living in the maze at Hampton Court!'

Nigel said rather startlingly, 'It isn't the physical mazes that ruin one – but the mental.'

'And emotional,' Max Faber added.

Carolyn's gaze met his. It struck her that, while he was not married, he had the air of a man who was accustomed to being with women. With that thought she decided that she was getting naïve. He probably had far more interest in, and experience of, women than any husband. She looked at Nigel, wondering if the word, emotional, would evoke any comment. His expression hardened. 'I'm rather tired of hearing that word; it is used to excuse every sexual indiscretion and abnormality.'

'I think the word *explain* might serve, also,' Max said.

Carolyn's voice was raised as she commented, 'How true that is. A reasonable explanation can prevent a very great deal of misery and misunderstanding.'

'That,' Nigel put in swiftly, 'depends on one's definition of reasonable. Some people have instinctive understanding; others understand only if every detail is hammered home first. But what are we doing standing here, talking like this?'

They returned to the sitting-room after

deciding that the study would make an excellent consulting room for Max Faber, who was delighted with the idea of having privacy and space in which to work. Carolyn intercepted a glance he exchanged with Nigel, and she felt shut out – almost as though these two shared a secret to which she was not privy. It was obvious that a great deal of negotiation must have gone on between them before tonight. As though aware of her gaze, Nigel plunged into almost banal conversation which she interrupted by saying, 'Most of the furniture in the study will have to be put in the loft.'

'I am afraid I am causing you inconvenience.'

'Not at all. We have never used this room. A dining room and sitting room are quite enough to cope with, plus, of course, Nigel's consulting room and surgery. But thank heaven, I think I may have found someone to live in. At least, Mrs Pringle, our daily help, has found her for me.'

Nigel said immediately, 'The first I've heard of it.'

She gave him a little secretive look, and ignored his remark as she went on, 'Things sometimes happen conveniently. This Mrs Mortimer is fifty and has worked in a doctor's household for the past ten years – since her husband died. She left because the family has gone to America and she did not fancy leaving England. I'm seeing her to-morrow. Since she knows Mrs Pringle there isn't likely to be any friction, or jealousy, between them. What is more, from my point of view, she loves cooking!'

'Sounds just what the doctor's wife ordered,' Max Faber said with a smile.

'Believe me it is,' Carolyn commented with fervour. She got up as she spoke, adding, 'I'll leave you to talk medicine to your heart's content. Goodnight, Doctor Faber.'

She went from the room, making her way across the hall and up the stairs as though in a trance. Suddenly the whole pattern of life at Downs Cottage had changed. Everything around her seemed unfamiliar, even the bed-room which she and Nigel shared. It was, she thought impersonally, a lovely room and the shades of delicate pink and blue enhanced its sensuous comfort. All her love and imagin-ation had gone into its furnishing, because she held the view that a bedroom betrayed the character of a woman more than any other room in the house, revealing her artistic sense, even her sexual desires. Sexual. Colour crept into her cheeks. Nigel seemed too tired to make love these days, and she had accepted the fact without allowing herself to dwell on its ultimate effect upon their marriage. Was this, she asked herself, how relationships started to disintegrate? Without drama, or any cataclysmic event; without even a bitter quarrel? She could not rid herself of the feeling that Nigel was being secretive far beyond the incidence of Max Faber's advent. Was there a new attraction – some patient with whom he had become involved? The idea struck a note of fantasy. He had never been a very demonstrative man. He rather despised any display of affection, regarding it as weakness, or insincerity. His silence could be eloquent, but not satisfying to anyone of her temperament. This was the first time she had allowed herself to take this phase of their relationship beyond the surface, while accepting the truth that she wanted to be seen as a woman, rather than as part of the furniture. It was like opening the door of an attic and tearing the cobwebs away from once cherished possessions, only to find those same possessions falling apart in the disillusionment of time. She sat down at her dressing table and stared at herself in the large oval mirror. There was no life in her expression, no light in her eyes; it was a face that had nothing to reflect except dissatisaction. She heard the voices faintly from the room below. And then, suddenly, Nigel's raised in anger. Or was that imagination? If Max Faber was annoying him now, what hope could there be for any partnership in the future? She listened intently, but the noise died down. The house took to itself an uneasy silence filled with suspense and unanswered questions.

Carolyn slipped quickly into the bath, pouring into it her favourite Lanvin cologne. While drying herself, she looked in the long panel of glass which covered part of one wall. Without conceit, she knew that she had a good figure, with firm breasts and a small waist. Her legs were long and slender and her skin was smooth and honey tinted, which made her body more voluptuous. She raised her arms and stretched them above her head. She could see the double bed through the open doorway and her pulse quickened as she recalled the nights when she and Nigel had lain there together, the world forgotten. She was so lost in reflection that it was not until Nigel appeared just outside the open bathroom door, that she realised his presence.

'Admiring yourself?' He spoke calmly.

Carolyn casually, and without haste, reached for her house-coat. She made no reply.

'You have a perfect figure,' he commented, as though appraising a statue. Then swiftly, 'You apparently approved of Faber. I'm glad.'

'If first appearances are anything to go by, he seems charming.' She walked into the bedroom as she spoke, and removing her house-coat, slid an attractive blue, French nylon nightdress over her head. Nigel was busy undressing, and as he went into the bathroom Carolyn got into bed. She was tense and alert. The words. 'You have a perfect figure', re-echoed, but hollowly. She waited, almost with apprehension, for him to come to bed. When he did so and switched off the light, he lay on his back beside her, his arm raised, his hand holding his head.

'You managed to get Mrs Mortimer pretty quickly.'

'To hear of her,' Carolyn corrected.

'She sounds ideal. Probably take over the running of the house completely.'

'As far as I wish her to do so.' Carolyn tried to keep her voice steady.

'What will she cost?'

'Not very much more than you pay Mrs Clark.'

'Mrs Clark is not fed,' he replied.

'Equally–' Carolyn's body heated in annoyance – 'with my doing the secretarial work for both you and Doctor Faber, the practice will be spared that expense. I take it that he will increase the income and add to the N.H.S. list, quite apart from cutting down your work.'

'Naturally. And is it your idea to be a philanthropist and not want a salary? I should have thought you were entitled to one.'

'Money doesn't come into it,' she answered. 'I merely want to do something which interests me. I thought you understood my attitude.'

'I do – perhaps too well.'

'And what is that supposed to mean?'

He turned over, his back towards her. 'I'm too tired to argue… Good night.'

To argue! Carolyn's heart was thumping. It seemed impossible to discuss anything without ending on a note of rancour. Loneliness overwhelmed her, for without any point of contact – not even a physical outlet – she might just as well be living with a stranger. She lay there listening to the wind howling and whining around the house. The mournful sound seemed a requiem to her own misery. Her eyes became attuned to the darkness so that she could pick out the objects of furniture that had been chosen so lovingly. Nigel was already lost to any problems, his breathing quietly regular. She envied him his ability to escape.

The telephone rang shrilly. Automatically Nigel, half asleep, answered it. 'Mrs *Wilder.*' That roused him from his blissful somnolent state. 'Vomiting.' He lifted himself slightly on his pillows. 'Why?' His voice was brusque. He added, impatiently, 'It is two o'clock in the morning, the roads are… Oh, you *do* know. Back from a party. Take some bicarbonate of soda. And another time take more water with your drinks,' he added gruffly. 'In fact cut drinking out altogether and give your liver a chance.' With that he rang off. 'Damn the woman. Just when I was in a good sleep. She's party mad. Max can take *her* over.' He spoke as though only half expecting Carolyn to answer. 'You asleep?'

'No; I can't sleep.'

He sighed drowsily. 'Don't tell me you'll be another one needing tablets.'

'An overdose most likely,' she exclaimed, hoping to rouse him so that he might turn towards her. But he made a little grunting sound, already dozing.

5

The routine at Downs Cottage changed completely during the following weeks. Mrs Mortimer became general factotum and proved to be cheerful and an excellent manager and cook. She and Mrs Pringle worked harmoniously together, and Carolyn was left free to do all the secretarial work of the practice, plus assisting either Nigel or Max Faber, when the necessity arose. On many occasions she was able to give injections and the status of 'the Doctor's wife' added to her authority. She took over the disused morning room as her office and in a very short while, had everything organised almost on hospital lines. She loved the work, seeing the patients, typing the reports and sliding back into medical terms as though her former nursing career had not been interrupted. She asked no concessions and certainly Nigel did not offer any. She could not fault him, but their relationship had lost its intimacy and his attitude was friendly, helpful, but detached. Nothing had been said about the change in the running of both the house and practice. It was only when Christmas approached that he dropped a little of his reserve and asked, 'What do you want to do this year? Have Christmas here?'

'We usually do,' she replied without challenge. 'Do you feel like going away?'

Nigel looked at Max. They had reached Christian name terms. 'How about you?'

'I might go to Dorset.'

'Dorset?' There was query in Nigel's voice. 'What part?'

'Sherborne. Do you know it?'

'I went to school there.'

Carolyn felt, once again, a strange suspicion as she watched the faces of the two men. She felt that Nigel was telling Max something he already knew. It struck her, also, that Max had hardly spoken of his background, and while all his particulars had obviously been submitted to the Sussex Executive Board and approved before Nigel could take him on (as an assistant with a view to partnership), his personal life remained a mystery. Her woman's intuition told her that there was some link between him and Nigel which both intended to conceal.

'You were lucky,' Max said, half enviously. 'You also have Cambridge degrees. I learned the hard way – in hospital.'

'Practical experience is worth a great deal of theory,' Nigel commented.

'I had my fill of it. Hospital promotion, half the time, means waiting for dead men's shoes, or a vacancy because someone else has managed to get higher up the graph. Trainee consultants are still underpaid and working well over a hundred hours a week. That was not for me.'

Nigel changed the subject. 'So you are going to Dorset for Christmas?'

Max lit a cigarette and said rather deliberately, 'Come to think of it, the hazards of our lovely winter, plus the travelling, makes Downs Cottage doubly attractive.' He looked around as he spoke. The soft lighting and flickering flames from the log-stacked fire brought a sensation of luxurious comfort. 'If I should not be intruding, I'd like to remain here, after all.' He shot Nigel an inscrutable smile. 'I can at least take over all the nuisance calls, with Mrs Wilder to top the list.'

Carolyn's voice betrayed her pleasure as she said, 'Oh, that would be fun.' She laughed. 'Not Mrs Wilder, but your remaining! You can help with the Christmas Eve party.'

'What party?' Nigel's brows puckered.

'The one I've decided to give. We owe hospitality to everyone.'

'Cocktail parties,' came the disgusted comment.

'Far more than that – a buffet affair. Mrs Mortimer is used to them.'

'Mrs Mortimer seems used to everything.'

'She is, thank heaven. I shall have a wonderful holiday. Be on strike from December 23rd.'

The door bell rang at that moment. They heard Mrs Mortimer answering it.

'I'll see to this,' Max said, getting to his feet.

'Good; I'm busy unless it is an emergency.'

Max reached the hall just as Moreen Fuller entered it. She stood for a second beneath the light, her face in shadow almost as though ashamed to be seen. Mrs Mortimer went quietly away.

'Can I help you?' Max moved so that he could see to whom he was talking. Moreen turned her gaze upon him and their eyes met. She was dazed and shaking as she cried out in alarm, 'Doctor Blake; I want Doctor Blake.'

Max caught her as she lurched forward and fainted.

Nigel, his ears attuned to every sound, heard his name called and rushed out into the hall.

Max muttered, as he carried the inert figure and placed it on the examining couch, 'I just managed to prevent her falling.'

'Get some brandy,' Nigel said swiftly, loosening the clothes at Moreen's neck. In that split second as he glanced up from his task, he was aware of the pallor of Max's face. 'Better have a drink yourself, you look as though you need it.'

A minute or so later, Moreen opened her eyes after Nigel had managed to get the glass to her lips. She gasped, her gaze appealing, '*You* ... not that – that stranger. *Please.*'

'Leave her to me,' Nigel said. 'Now,' he added, as the door closed on Max, 'one more sip.' He held the glass to her lips again. 'Lie quietly for a minute.'

Her expression was agitated. Despite the faintness she was unable to rest. 'My father knows.' Her words tumbled out in pathetic jerks. She raised herself against the pillow. 'I didn't think it showed, but he noticed I'd put on weight and that I didn't look well.' She rushed on, 'When he accused me, I couldn't lie. Then he went mad. I've never seen him in a rage before. It was terrible. He wanted to know the name of the man. When I wouldn't tell him–' She covered her face with her hands. 'I grabbed a coat and ran out of the house without being seen.' Her eyes were staring, hunted. 'I had to talk to you, Doctor. And when–' She raised her gaze and lowered it, 'seeing a stranger when I got here ... the cold and everything. I'm sorry about fainting.'

Nigel studied her intently. He was accustomed to the contradictory pattern of pregnancy, and its effect upon both personality and behaviour, but even allowing for Moreen's reaction to her father's anger, there was something about her manner that puzzled him.

'You couldn't help fainting and Doctor Faber, who prevented your falling, is now working with me in the practice. He certainly will not be a stranger.'

'You are the only doctor I want to see,' she insisted on a note of near-hysteria.

Nigel ignored her remark by asking, 'And your aunt? You said you could go to her.'

'I was wrong. She can't have me. I thought I could go for Christmas, plan something. She doesn't want to be mixed up in it. Her daughter – my cousin – is my age. She spoke of a bad influence and it being embarrassing because Dick – her son – would be there. Dick's nice; he wouldn't condemn anyone.' Tears rolled down her cheeks and seemed more poignant because she made no sound.

All Nigel said was, 'I'm glad your father knows. Now I can talk to him.'

She shook her head. 'There's nothing to talk about.'

'There's everything to discuss and to plan.' A cold disgust touched him as he thought of the aunt. 'Believe me, Moreen, he will help you when it comes to it. The first shock … you've got to see his point of view.'

'I still won't tell him what he wants to know.' She was shaking as she spoke, agitation, fear and a terror of the unknown, making her head spin, her nerves like a violin string about to snap. 'He'll ring at any moment. I know he will, and I don't know what to do.' She gave a shuddering sigh. 'What to *do*,' she repeated with tragic emphasis.

The telephone rang. It was Malcolm Fuller, distraught, almost incoherent. Nigel deliberately sounded matter of fact, finishing with, 'By all means come and fetch her.' As Nigel replaced the receiver he wondered just how many times a day he heard the words, 'I must talk to you'. An irrelevant thought chased through his mind. To whom could *he* talk?

Moreen said, 'I wish he wouldn't come. I can't argue and fight any more.'

Nigel studied her with compassion. She looked so young, so helpless. Tragedy was written all over her face, and her eyes were dark smudges concealing a secret her lips would not divulge. It was not an unfamiliar pattern. In some cases time and difficulties weakened resolution; in others it strengthened determination.

'You won't have to; leave things to me.'

She said quietly, 'You'd respect my reasons all the more if I could tell you the truth.'

'I'm sure I should. I hope he's worthy of all this heartache.'

Her eyes had the look of suffering that was

timeless, and when she spoke, she might have been speaking for all women. 'Love doesn't weigh up worthiness. I know that now.' She added in a voice unlike her own in its quietness and resignation, 'Even if I'd been older, I don't suppose it would have made any difference... I feel very old suddenly – and strange. You've been so good, so patient with me, Doctor.'

He smiled at her, but he was troubled. He was dealing with someone to whom, despite her years, comforting phrases would not be acceptable. It was not merely a question of pregnancy with which he was confronted, but with unhappiness and desperate hurt.

'You just rest there and don't do any more talking. Come now, lie down and be good,' he finished, with a half smile.

She submitted silently and lay back, closing her eyes. There was no colour in her cheeks, and her dark lashes lay upon them like a thick fringe. Nigel put a blanket over her and went quietly back to the sitting-room.

'What happened?' Max spoke anxiously.

'Fainting isn't uncommon in pregnancy.'

'Pregnancy...' He sounded shattered. 'Good lord, she only looks a child herself. Silly remark,' he hastened.

'I'm letting her sleep for a few minutes – until her father comes to collect her.'

Carolyn got up from her chair. 'If she

shouldn't be asleep, she might like a hot drink. I won't disturb her,' she added swiftly. 'I'm an adept at opening doors quietly.' Her sigh was eloquent of concern. 'I don't envy you having to tackle Mr Fuller.'

Mr Fuller arrived five minutes later. 'She's all right?' The words were his form of greeting.

Nigel led him into the dining-room so that they could talk alone.

'I lost my temper, Doctor.' Malcolm Fuller was a thin, worrying type of man, whose manner was usually gentle. He was liked and respected by the towns-folk, and his devotion – as distinct from possessiveness – to his children was an example to all parents. 'It wasn't because of the baby,' he rushed on, 'the shock; and Moreen protecting him. I'd do anything for her happiness, set them up in a flat, or a house – help–' He made a gesture to convey his frustration. 'But if she won't even tell this man of her condition–' His expression was a mute appeal for guidance.

'Marriage is very often the worst solution unless the circumstances are right.'

'You think he's married already?' It was a sentence that came breathlessly and in fear. 'I was wrong to lose my temper; she just ran out without my knowing, and I've been almost demented. What can I *do?*'

'Stand by her and ask no questions. She

will tell you in her own time – but not now.'

The man slumped in his chair. 'Of course I'll stand by her, but this will ruin her whole future. You know she wanted to be a nurse?'

'She has time on her side for that.' Nigel paused before adding, 'At the moment all she needs is understanding, and the affection you have always given her. You are her only security – emotionally and physically. I'm seeing these cases every day, Mr Fuller, and all too often they happen to the very nicest people.' As he spoke, Nigel poured out a whisky. 'Drink this,' he said quietly, 'then I am going to get your daughter. Will you let me do the talking?'

Malcolm Fuller nodded and murmured, 'Gladly.'

'But you must make her understand that you are not condemning her. I know how difficult it all is and I do not under-estimate all you are going through, but unless we can convince her that this isn't the end of the world–' Nigel stopped abruptly. He met a wide, staring, even horrified gaze, 'You don't think she'd take her life? I mean–' The words seemed to choke him.

'We have to make this situation as painless as possible in order to prevent any question of that.'

Nigel went into the consulting room; Moreen was stirring from a brief sleep. She sat up in consternation. Nigel explained that her father was there and she instinctively shrank from the idea of seeing him. Nevertheless she walked beside Nigel to the dining-room and there, rather like a homing pigeon, went straight to her father's outstretched arms, cradling her head on his shoulder and clinging to him as though afraid he would vanish. 'I'm sorry,' he whispered, 'that I lost my temper. I won't ask any more questions.'

'I'll tell you,' she murmured, 'when I can.'

Nigel said without preliminaries, 'Do you still want to keep the baby?' He watched her expression carefully.

She did not hesitate. 'No.' Her voice was firm. 'I've changed my mind. I want it adopted!'

6

Downs Cottage came to life during Christmas week. Carolyn refused to allow depression to spoil her enthusiasm for the party, and Max proved to be a gay ally, maintaining that he enjoyed all celebrations because they broke the monotony of day-to-day living. He assisted in decorating the Christmas tree (which rose from the floor almost to the ceiling), nearly falling off the steps as he put the glittering star on the top branch. He also managed to get the fairy lights going so that Nigel, coming in and seeing the flashing, multi-coloured bulbs, said, 'Good lord; they went phut last year and I forgot all about them! Must say that everywhere looks marvellous and the balloons hung like that make it all most professional.' He glanced at Carolyn, whose face was flushed with eager delight. 'In your element.' His voice was encouraging.

'I always have loved Christmas,' Carolyn said. 'I wish my parents were alive to come and stay. Sad, really, that neither Nigel nor I have any close relations left. Orphans of the storm.' She forced a little laugh. 'I was brought up in a riotous home, and we went mad at Christmas.'

Max was standing back meditating whether the star was at just the right angle. Then he said, 'I had the most dreary Christmases possible. My father and mother regarded it as a nuisance and an extravagance. They believed in strength through misery. Their religion certainly did not inspire me to follow in their footsteps... Now I think all we need is one more lantern on that lower branch. Looks a bit lop-sided otherwise.'

Carolyn handed him the only lantern left.

'How about a drink?' Nigel suggested.

Carolyn nodded. 'Drink break, Max. My shoes are full of feet!'

Nigel disappeared and returned with a bottle of champagne. Mrs Mortimer brought in the glasses, and joined in the first drink before hurrying away to attend to the meal.

Carolyn lay back in her chair and sighed, well pleased. 'No cooking and no washing up,' she said blithely. 'I've enjoyed every moment of this day.'

'So have I,' Max agreed. He looked at Nigel. 'Now you're off until after the holiday. All the patients are my pigeons and if they do not like it, they can go unattended! A few are bound to cook up some trivial thing just as the turkey goes on the table.' He grinned. 'Remember the emergency take-ins on Christmas day?' Carolyn noticed how quickly he added, 'I'll bet it was the same where you trained.'

'Just the same,' Nigel replied. 'Not bad champagne.'

'The gift of a grateful patient,' Carolyn teased.

'Ah!' Max gave a little secretive smile. 'All visits are not unpleasant.'

'Which reminds me,' Carolyn exclaimed, not allowing herself to be involved in the pointed comment, 'Freda's bringing along a friend of hers who has just joined a practice in Hove. A glamorous doctor – female. Anita Benson.'

The sudden silence was electric; a silence which Nigel broke, his voice too casual, 'Just as long as she is glamorous – fine.' He added. 'I've never heard Freda speak of her.'

'She has spoken of her to me.' Carolyn's heart quickened its beat as suspicion filled her mind. 'You have seen so little of Freda and David lately that it is a wonder you even remember their names.' Her laughter was unnatural and she glanced at Max, intercepting a look he flashed at Nigel.

Max said, as he raised his champagne glass to his lips, 'I seem to recollect the name.'

'Anita is hardly a common one,' Carolyn persisted.

'But Doctor Benson,' Nigel added, 'is not *un*common.'

'Amazing,' Max went on, 'how quickly one

forgets even people with whom one once worked. I suppose the numbers account for it. In medical circles, I must say, the arm of coincidence seems longer than in any other.'

'And professional secrecy,' Carolyn said with faint cynicism, 'the habit that lingers almost to become a vice in private life. Then it always savours of a guilty conscience.'

Max laughed. 'I assure you I have no guilty conscience where Doctor Benson is concerned – always assuming that my memory is not at fault.'

'It probably will be,' Nigel suggested. He filled up their glasses and fumbled for his cigarette case. Carolyn handed it to him.

'Ah, always losing the darn thing.'

'I must get you just a packet next time,' she said, without malice.

He smiled rather weakly, looking absent minded. The gay atmosphere vanished, like air from a pricked balloon. 'I'd hate that... This room looks enormous now that you've denuded it of half the furniture.'

Carolyn forced herself back into a semblance of light-heartedness. 'We can dance in here – carpet, or no carpet.'

'Corrupting the medical profession,' Max said with a wry smile.

'Impossible!' She grinned at him. 'You're all shockers. And don't contradict me. I was a nurse.'

'And don't tell me you shrank from the

fun,' he countered.

'To be honest, no! The crushes, the moods of ecstasy followed by a deep depression over Iceland. And still we found ourselves standing at the altar, with our happiness in their hands – not our lives! Although it could almost be the same thing.'

'That reminds me!' Max exclaimed, 'the mistletoe. We haven't put it up in the hall.'

Nigel felt irritated by the constant use of the word 'we'. He said, when he and Carolyn were alone, 'Max certainly seems to have made himself at home.'

She stared, baffled. 'Since he is living here, it would be pretty uncomfortable had he not done so.'

'As long as you approve.'

'I'm thankful he's sociable. Patients like him. Are you not satisfied?'

'He's doing his job well.'

Carolyn fixed Nigel with a look of inquiry. 'And you knew him before he came to stay at Alfriston.'

Nigel started, jerking his head up, his expression wary. 'What makes you suggest that?'

'Call it woman's intuition.' She continued to watch him closely. To her surprise he said, 'I would prefer not to discuss the matter.'

Carolyn felt shut out, but she murmured, 'Very well.'

Carollers began to sing at that moment.

She heard Max go to the door and immediately joined him. 'Do you know "Silent Night"?' Carolyn looked at the red-cheeked faces with an indulgent affection. Their breath puffed out into the frosty night air, emphasising the cold. The youngest boy among the five piped up, 'I know it – they know it, too.' Whereupon they all sang lustily, delighted to be taken notice of, and not shooed away like so many chickens, as was all too often the case.

'My favourite, too,' Carolyn half whispered to Max.

Nigel crossed the hall and stood at Carolyn's side. He had brought three of the children into the world and knew their families; they grinned at him as they sang.

When the door finally closed on them, the spirit of goodwill had returned. Nigel glanced up at the mistletoe which Max had hung conspicuously beneath the centre light. He drew Carolyn to him and kissed her. It was a friendly kiss which she returned.

'May I?' Max spoke as Carolyn and Nigel moved apart.

'No law against it,' Nigel said with a laugh.

Max leaned forward and kissed Carolyn's cheek, lingering just a fraction of a second. She tensed at his touch, aware of a sudden and exciting physical contact which made her cautiously move away. She avoided looking at him and made some inaudible remark about seeing how long dinner would be, as she went into the kitchen.

Mrs Mortimer was in process of dishing up, her cheeks flushed and her eyes bright. She was happy and thankful to have found a home in which she was free to plan to the best of her ability, without interference or criticism.

'Just ready,' she said brightly. 'The champagne nearly went to my head!'

Carolyn looked at her with genuine affection. Every day she was thankful for her presence, her unobtrusive manner, and skill in running the house without making her, Carolyn, feel a cypher in it.

'Curry,' Mrs Mortimer went on brightly. 'Doctor loves it.'

'Not only Doctor,' Carolyn spoke with enthusiasm. 'I love it too. But it was a fiddly meal to choose when you have so much to do. I never could make a proper curry.' She moved as she spoke, surveying the long, wide formica-topped shelf which was laden with sausage rolls and mince pies – everything possible to prepare in advance.

'The lobster patties and canapés Mrs Pringle and I can do in the morning,' Mrs Mortimer observed calmly. 'Things must be fresh.' As she spoke she fluffed the rice around the curry dish.

'I'll round up the medical profession,' Carolyn exclaimed, 'or they'll disappear into the attic the moment they know the meal is on the table!' She went out of the kitchen and reached the sitting room door which was ajar. In that moment she heard Max say rather impatiently, 'You've no need to fear that I shall betray anything.'

Carolyn backed away, feeling slightly sick. Then, humming out of tune, walked quickly into the room saying, with forced gaiety, 'The meal is just about to be put on the table. Better do your disappearing act quickly.' She was conscious of the uneasy, almost beady, expression on Nigel's face; an expression that changed into a weak, tentative smile.

The dining-room was bright with holly on which were masses of shining red berries. A miniature Christmas tree sparkled in the centre of the table. Carolyn said involuntarily as they began to eat, 'One needs children to bring this festivity to life.' For a second Nigel's gaze met hers and fell away in embarrassment. She could not help a cold criticism flashing into her eyes. Just what was he concealing? She had genuinely believed that there had been complete frankness between them when they married, accepting the fact that he had enjoyed several sexual relationships. In fairness to him, he had not tried to deceive her on that score. Now the suspicion engendered by his attitude brought a sense of bereavement.

The following evening arrived and she made a resolution to enjoy every moment of it, almost as though she were a guest. The house could not have looked more attractive, or festive; the food was perfect and the dining-table groaned under the weight of delicacies that had, seemingly miraculously, appeared from the kitchen. Nigel had hired two waiters and improvised a bar so that people could order their own drinks, and not have to take semi-warm, watered cocktails from trays which seemed always to be at the other side of the room when the crush was greatest.

Max, alone with Carolyn before the door bell went for the first time said, 'This is magnificent and if I may say so, your dress is most glamorous. I like that shiny, sleek look. You are a fascinating woman, Carolyn. No apologies for the compliment which is a statement of fact.' He held her gaze. 'But you have a Gioconda smile that is both baffling and irresistible. Fire and ice describes you.'

Carolyn was acutely conscious of him as he stood beside her. She was the last woman to be deceived by flattering words, and usually ignored them. His expression made that almost impossible. Her voice was smooth and far more controlled than she felt. 'I prefer fire,' she retorted flippantly. 'I am intrigued by the ice.' It struck her that it was a pleasant change even to talk nonsense that embraced herself. She had begun to feel rather like a statistic, a newspaper, and a case sheet.

'So am I.' His smile was a challenge. 'Ah, the first to arrive!'

'That's Freda's ring.'

Nigel came downstairs just as Carolyn opened the front door, greeting Freda and David with an artificial gaiety, and then facing Anita Benson with a welcoming smile.

Freda laughed. 'Anita is bringing coals to Newcastle. Three doctors in the house.'

There was a moment of dramatic silence during which time Carolyn saw Anita Benson's gaze rest upon Nigel with a faintly familiar, possessive air, and having made a few polite remarks, said, 'I've heard a great deal about you, Doctor Blake. In fact I think we may have met at some time or another.'

Anita Benson was fair, with china blue eyes that could be deceptive in their apparent frankness. She was a determined type, accustomed to having her own way. What passed for kindness was, too often, calculating selfishness. She studied Carolyn with a faintly patronising air. 'Two doctors in the house all the time must be pretty wearing... Or perhaps one sees them with a different eye when working in hospital with them.'

Carolyn flashed back, 'Having been a nurse, I appreciate what you mean.'

Max chalked up a score to Carolyn. He had no effusive greeting for Anita whom he recognised, regarding her presence as a danger, as well as a challenge.

David put an arm about Carolyn's shoulder and propelled her towards the mistletoe. 'Before the queue starts,' he laughed.

Carolyn relaxed. David and she were good friends, and the thought struck her that he was the type of man to whom she would instinctively turn in trouble. She kissed him with spontaneous affection. Nigel said hurriedly, 'Let's get a first drink in before anyone else arrives... Freda, that dress makes you look very alluring.'

Freda raised her hand and felt his forehead.

'What's that in aid of?'

'Just to make sure you are not running a temperature.'

Anita gave a little laugh. 'Meaning that compliments do not come readily from Doctor Blake? May I call you Nigel? I shall remember where we met if you give me time.'

Freda frowned. The under-current did not escape her.

Carolyn led the way into the sitting-room. 'Most ungallant of my husband not to recall having met you, Doctor Benson... Nigel, I think champagne is good to start off with.'

Max edged to Freda's side. She smiled up

at him, wondering how things were working out, and convinced that Carolyn had a great deal to conceal these days. 'Everywhere looks marvellous,' she said. 'Carolyn has a genius for making a house seem ten times better than anyone else's – even when it comes to decorations.'

Carolyn heard the remark. 'Much of this is Max's handiwork. We had great fun yesterday putting the decorations up.'

They gathered in semi-circle at the bar where a waiter dispensed the drinks.

'This bottle,' Nigel said, taking the champagne from the ice bucket, 'I will open in honour of special friends.'

'That,' said Anita softly, 'is a charming gesture.' She made it sound as if *she* was the special friend, and a little inscrutable smile touched her lips as she looked up into Nigel's face.

Nigel concentrated on uncorking the bottle and when the glasses were filled, he inclined his head and said, 'To a good evening.'

Anita's attitude roused Carolyn's jealousy, even her fear. She knew that she must not betray either, and was grateful for Max's moral support. He stimulated the conversation by telling stories about his search for the right flat, or house, and the humorous incidents that had occurred.

Nigel said laughingly, 'The truth is that

Max has no objections to Downs Cottage!'

David spoke more for the sake of talking than anything else. He sensed that all was not well in the household, without being able to put his finger on what was wrong. 'Which shows Doctor Faber's good taste.'

Max looked slightly uncomfortable. He was reluctant to admit how happy he had been since joining the practice, particularly on account of his growing regard for Carolyn. 'I could not,' he said, 'deny either of those statements.'

Nigel was looking at Anita. She stood, glass raised, and met his gaze. Her toast to him was obvious by her intimate half-smile. An imperceptible silence fell. Freda could not remember such an atmosphere in the house before. She plunged into a series of what she knew to be inanities, incapable even of feeling any excitement at the prospect of the evening ahead. In addition, she could not understand Anita's attitude. She and Anita had been friends for some years, but it was one of those relationships interspersed with absence, during which time the telephone had served as a link. It had come as a surprise when Anita had moved from London and given up her appointment at the hospital to join a practice in Hove. It struck Freda that there was nothing coincidental about the remark regarding Nigel. Instinct told her that they had known each other in the past, and that the last thing Nigel wished was that she should be there at the moment. At that point Freda's curiosity vanished. She did not want to know anything calculated to hurt Carolyn. David glanced at her with the understanding intimacy natural to two people who were married and still in love. Words were not necessary, even could they have been uttered.

The house filled up; patients from the surrounding districts; friends from considerable distances; a few relations, and many hospital colleagues. The party gathered momentum; voices babbled in wave after wave of sound and laughter. Carolyn saw that everyone circulated instead of getting together in neat little groups. The bar thrived under Nigel's continual hospitality. Women of all ages clustered around him, some with obvious crushes, their eyes gazing into his as though he were a film star; others relating all possible anecdotes about their children, grandchildren – and inevitably their own ailments, which he skilfully managed to avoid discussing! Max supported him and was a great asset. Every now and then he managed to slide between the scented bodies and speak to Carolyn, one eye on Anita in case she should choose to use the occasion for her own ends.

'It's going marvellously,' he murmured.

Carolyn nodded. 'Judging by the noise, it

couldn't be better... Get me a special Martini, Max.'

He held her gaze for a second, then returned to her side and handed her the glass. He raised his own. 'I'd like to think that this Christmas Eve may be the first of many we enjoy together ... thank you for making me so welcome here, Carolyn. It could have been very uncomfortable had you been a different type. When I get my own home I shall be able to entertain you.' He added, 'That is, providing Nigel finally accepts me as his partner.'

Carolyn looked surprised to the point of concern. 'Why shouldn't he accept you?'

'We both have the privilege of changing our mind about the association.'

She said swiftly, 'I'd hate to start this all over again with someone new whom I disliked.'

There was a significant pause before he said, 'That encourages me to believe that, at least, you do not dislike me, or even that I am regarded as a—'

'A what?' Anita exclaimed, having crept through a mass of people to reach their side in time to hear the last few words of the conversation.

Carolyn forced a smile. 'You have excellent hearing above all this noise... Your glass is empty.'

Max took the glass and had it re-filled.

Damn the woman, he thought fiercely.

Carolyn said briefly, 'I can see a newcomer ... forgive me.' She hurried away.

'What,' asked Max, 'made you come to this part of the world?' He stared Anita out as he spoke, and his voice was anything but polite.

'It's a free country,' she retorted. 'What are you worried about?'

'Your tongue,' he answered sharply.

Her laughter tinkled, but was without mirth.

'You have nothing to worry about.'

'Precisely; there are more ways of killing a cat—'

She laughed again. Max thought that no one could deny her attractiveness. She had a subtle sex appeal which she knew how to use; just as she knew her own power, and the lengths to which she could go in order to achieve her objective. 'You are a strange man. In the circumstances—'

'I do not need reminding of what you glibly call "the circumstances".' Max raised his voice. 'Neither have I forgotten your brilliant contribution to them.'

She ignored that. 'I am intrigued to find you working here with Nigel. I wonder if his wife knows all the facts.'

Nigel escaped from a colleague and edged his way towards them. He hoped he did not appear as grey as he felt. The sight of Max and Anita together unnerved him. The ghost of the past hovered avengingly and he was afraid of the consequences. How far could he trust Max? He had no illusions about Anita's attractive persuasiveness, or its effect upon even the strongest character.

Max made an elaborate move towards a young patient who was trying to attract his attention, leaving Nigel to face Anita who looked straight into his eyes and said softly, 'It is so wonderful to see you. It has seemed centuries since we–' She paused deliberately.

'A great deal has happened since then. My marriage, for instance.'

Her question was direct. 'Rebound, Nigel?'

His voice was tinged with anger. 'No. Nothing of the kind.'

'You annoyance seems too defensive to be genuine. Surely we can do without pretence.'

He lit a cigarette, his nerves tingling.

'Did you know I was practising here? I can hardly believe it was coincidence.'

'The medical register is very comprehensive. No, my coming here is not coincidence. I thought Lewes would be too obvious... Hove is near enough – and far enough away. A convenient compromise.'

'Look here, Anita, I want you to understand one thing quite clearly–'

'That you are a happily married man? I

should take a great deal of convincing on that score. You certainly don't look it, and your wife – when she is not talking to anyone and putting on an act – seems very much on edge. There's no gaiety between you. I'd say that Max is her attraction.'

'Don't be ridiculous,' he snapped.

'Very well; women sense things.'

'When it suits them,' he retorted.

She gave a little laugh that was not unfriendly. 'I see no reason why she should not enjoy his company. He is a very attractive man..... Nigel are you sorry to see me?'

He did not hesitate. 'Yes; very.' His expression was grave.

'Nostalgia?'

'Remembrance can be painful.' He could not avoid her persistent gaze.

'So I mean enough for that?'

'Do you seriously imagine I could forget all that happened? Heaven knows I've tried.'

She spoke quietly, 'Emotion and discipline seldom go together. I must talk to you.' She fumbled in her bag as she spoke and surreptitiously slipped her card into his hand, but not before Carolyn – who was standing a little distance away – had seen the gesture. 'Come next Wednesday about five,' Anita whispered.

Nigel put the card in his pocket. 'I think it would be a good idea for me to make you understand exactly the position. For that reason, and that reason only, I'll come. We can hardly talk above this din, or with curious eyes upon us.'

Anita did not mind what reason he gave, so long as she could see him alone. She flashed him a little intimate smile and linked up with Carolyn.

'I was right, Mrs Blake. I have met your husband before. We trained at the Princess Ann together.'

7

Carolyn tried to be self-possessed as she met Anita's smiling eyes. Thoughts chased through her mind with the rapidity of a forest fire. Was Anita the answer to Nigel's aloofness; the reason for his secrecy?

'The ever recurring coincidence,' Carolyn said smoothly... 'Have you been in Hove long?'

'A matter of weeks.'

Carolyn was not the type to delude herself. Here was a woman who would attract men, and not, automatically, alienate women. Had Nigel and she been lovers? And what was written on the card she had given him? Her address? Whatever it was built up suspicion. Was Freda aware of any link between Nigel and her? If so, it was out of character for Freda to be party to any deception.

Max, hovering, and trying to talk to as many guests as possible, while still keeping an eye on Anita, could do nothing just then to break up the conversation between her and Carolyn. He was thankful when Carolyn invited everyone into the dining-room where the buffet awaited them. His collar, by this time, felt two sizes smaller than

113

when he put it on. Passing Nigel (as Nigel was about to help an aged patient) he murmured, 'For God's sake man, smile. This is supposed to be a party, not an execution.' Nigel snapped some unintelligible words back, and after a while gave his attention to Mrs Philips who was standing hesitantly at the table, looking at the beautifully arranged food for which she had no appetite.

'It's a wonderful evening, Doctor. And so good of your wife to have invited me.' She paused because she was not sure if she dare mention personal matters, but then said in a breath, 'It will be a strange Christmas without him.' Her eyes asked the question her lips dare not utter.

'He has made progress, Mrs Philips. If anything can help him in this fight it is the knowledge of what happened to you when he was drunk that last night.'

She nodded. 'I wish I could be hard. Life's so much easier that way.'

Nigel studied her with compassion. She was a woman condemned to the torture of hope and fear. Hope that the alcoholic might recover and take his place among normal men; and fear of *being afraid* should this happen, only to prove a temporary remission and, thus, plunge her back into greater torment. He said, gently, 'Easier, perhaps; but without so much that is worth while.'

'He looks better.' She might not have

heard Nigel's words. 'If it were just an illness – even an incurable one – I could take care of him.' She looked apologetic. 'It is very wrong of me to speak of all this now... Your house is just as I should have imagined it knowing your wife. She has been kind to me.'

Nigel felt a pang because of his own helplessness. This frail woman, still attractive and in her early thirties, had been cheated of life in all its phases, by a man cursed with a disease that could be far worse than many regarded with horror, and listed in medical books as incurable. The thought flashed through his mind how much kinder death could be than this twilight of living. At the moment she was neither wife, nor widow, tied to a human wreck. Not being able to give her his undivided attention, Nigel made certain that she had cheerful acquaintances around her, and then turned his attention to Freda for a few seconds, finding her gaze somewhat disconcerting in its silent questioning. Anita insinuated herself between them, her plate well laden. She had an enormous appetite and made no secret of the fact that she was greedy over food. It was, in fact, a general characteristic.

'Nigel used to tease me about the food I could consume,' she said brightly, addressing Freda and conscious of her reserved expression. 'Mrs Mortimer is certainly a wonderful cook, and seems always to be in the right place at the right moment. I've been watching her. Such service is rare to get these days.'

Freda did not realise that there was a belligerent note in her voice as she said, 'Carolyn is a wonderful cook, too, and she has a flair for getting people to do everything for her. A great achievement.'

Anita smiled blandly, 'How I agree with the word "achievement".'

Later, Carolyn, having avoided Nigel as far as possible during the evening, caught up with him for a few seconds while the guests were busy eating. He looked at her uncertainly, wondering what Anita might have said. To his relief she spoke normally. 'Mrs Mortimer has certainly proved an expert at this sort of thing. It is quite a change to enjoy my own party without starting in a state of exhaustion.'

'I'm glad you're pleased.'

She met his gaze. 'And you?'

'I'm looking forward to the moment when it's all over.'

Carolyn wondered if that was merely a discreet statement. She had no intention of mentioning Anita, or making an issue of her presence there. 'Max has been a great asset.' As she spoke she glanced across the room to a spot where Max was standing engrossed in conversation with a striking auburn-haired girl of about nineteen. 'I cannot place her.'

'Julie Fielding.'

'Ah, of course! It must be the drinks. The actress! And I was determined to have a talk with her – having heard you mention her so often. Most fascinating.'

'Apparently Max finds her so, judging by his expression.' As he spoke, Nigel recalled Anita's words about Max being the attraction where Carolyn was concerned.

'Which shows his good taste,' Carolyn exclaimed.

Nigel felt on edge as he waited for her to mention Anita. While he was grateful for her attitude of friendliness, he distrusted her silence as being unnatural, and then consoled himself with the fact that this was hardly the time, or place, to begin any discussion. The explanation, however, did not satisfy him. He met Max's glance at that second and a worried look was exchanged between them. Nigel hated the babble around him, and was aware of Anita's predatory gaze seeming to follow him no matter how he tried to escape from it. He was relieved when Carolyn left him and it was no longer necessary for him to try to think of the right thing to say – and the wrong thing to avoid.

From the point of view of giving a very successful party, the night could not have pleased the guests more. Hilarity built up once the dancing began and, as Carolyn had said, 'carpet or no carpet' they danced until the early hours, to the music of the stereophonic radiogram.

Carolyn danced with Max, emotion stirring as he held her gaze. For a while she forgot Nigel and Anita, and felt the thrill of excitement as Max said softly, 'I'm glad the ice has melted, Carolyn.'

A tremor went over her and she asked involuntarily, 'What kind of a man are you?' She emphasised the word 'kind'.

His gaze remained steady. 'Are you thinking morally?'

'I suppose,' she admitted honestly, 'I was.' She felt his hand tighten on hers.

'I suppose I've had as much experience as the average man. I'm no saint, Carolyn.' His voice changed and a note of regret crept into it. 'There are one or two things I'd like to wipe out, but unfortunately there's no such thing as putting back the clock.' A wry smile touched his lips. 'So far, I've never really been in love – whatever the term may mean. Sex; emotion – yes. Both, I'm beginning to think, need a proper framework.'

'No escape for Don Juan.' She tried to sound provocative but, to her dismay, she realised that she was involved with what had been said. It brought an intimacy which awakened a desire that she did not try to deny. She was not impressionable, but there was something about Max's attitude that emphasised the emptiness of her present married life. The last thing she wanted was any complicated relationship, yet the fact that they had been able to communicate made her feel suddenly alive.

Max prompted, 'Do you agree with my views?'

She echoed his words, 'a proper framework,' and said unsteadily, 'Meaning marriage?'

'I suppose so.'

'That sounds reluctant.' Her heart quickened its beat.

'Perhaps it is. Marriage is not always simple.' His gaze held hers and emotion stirred between them.

The music stopped at that second and she heard Nigel's voice whispering in her ear, 'I think it's about time we broke all this up.'

'Why?'

'It's Christmas Day.' Nigel shot Max a critical look.

Carolyn stood amid the laughter, suddenly isolated from it. Only the lights from the sparkling tree illuminated the room, and the festive spirit was rather like a giant wave defying the tide. Freda, quick to sense Nigel's mood, made the first move to break the party up. Greetings were exchanged; more laughter; genuine thanks, and the gradual departure of the guests amid the sounds of cars being started up, engines revving to combat the cold, until the house became silent as the front door shut.

Max took up a position at the foot of the stairs. Desire had to give priority to discretion. 'Good night,' he said, keeping a bright note in his voice. 'And thank you again for a wonderful evening.' With that he turned and made his way to his room.

Nigel's nerves were taut, his temper frayed. He could not cope with, or analyse, his emotions. 'Another ordeal over,' he exclaimed.

Carolyn refused to allow him to damp her enthusiasm. 'I enjoyed every second of it,' she said stoutly.

'So I noticed.'

'A wet blanket hostess is about as stimulating as a sexless man.' The words rushed out.

Nigel flashed, 'You seem very preoccupied with sex these days.'

They reached the edge of the precipice as she retorted, 'Which is more than can be said of you... Or am I being naïve?'

They faced each other trembling with anger; his conflict and her frustration declaring war between them; a war neither wanted. The shadow of Anita lay between them. Carolyn craved his confidence and he hoped for her comment. In addition, he considered that Max had been far too attentive to her –

obviously without rebuff.

Carolyn glanced at the clock. A pang went through her as she thought of the holiday ahead. As she walked to the door she said in a subdued voice, 'I promised David and Freda we would have drinks with them on Boxing morning.'

Nigel jerked his head up, instantly alert. 'Why?'

'Seeing that we've always done so, isn't that rather an odd remark? Or have you suddenly taken a dislike to them, too?'

'Now you are being ridiculous.' Why didn't she mention Anita? He asked himself the question again.

'This whole thing is ridiculous… Anyway, I'm tired.' She thought of Max as she went up to bed. She was neither tired, nor sleepy. His words, 'There's no such thing as putting back the clock', aroused her interest as well as curiosity. And what were the things he would like to wipe out? Since he had, on his own admission, never really been in love, it could mean only affairs. With whom? Did Anita figure in his past? She retreated from the idea, and yet felt that in some way Anita was destined to play a considerable part in their future. Why, also, her thoughts raced on, should Max not have mentioned training at the Princess Ann when he knew that it was where Nigel also trained? And more important, why had Nigel himself not referred to it?

Nigel came up to bed just as she was sliding between the sheets. He avoided her gaze and began to undress in silence. What, Carolyn asked herself, had made him speak of her being preoccupied with sex these days? She could not recall having mentioned the word to him, his coldness precluding any such reference. Was that his way of making it clear he had no further interest in the physical side of their marriage? Her body heated at the possibility. He had nothing to fear as far as she was concerned. Nevertheless the memory of their conversation disturbed her. It was a straw in the wind of what was fast becoming a bleak, sterile relationship.

She felt the warmth of his body beside her, and tensed as he switched off the light. Would he touch her, reach for her hand? She knew that one move and she would be in his arms, passion dulling suspicion because desire was paramount. But he moved only to turn away.

She hated herself because tears filled her eyes, and a great hunger became part of yearning.

It was a Christmas day she was destined never to forget.

8

Carolyn returned to work after Christmas was over and felt a great sense of relief because it was no longer necessary to try to keep up the exhausting pretence of being gay.

A full surgery seemed a blessing, the patients diagnosing their own complaints with the help of knowledge gained from television. The word enteritis cropped up with monotonous regularity, with seldom the confession of overeating. Carolyn steered the sufferers into the respective consulting rooms, assisting both Nigel and Max as, and when, they needed it. Nigel behaved as he would have done to any secretary employed; Max with greater deference, but with considerably more intimacy which manifested itself in the occasional glances he gave her, and in the tone of his voice.

Malcolm Fuller was the last patient. Nigel had been called out to an angina case, and Carolyn said, a little startled as she saw him sitting alone in the surgery, 'I'm afraid my husband has been called out to a heart case, Mr Fuller. Perhaps Doctor Faber might help... Ah,' as Max joined her, 'here is

Doctor Faber.'

Malcolm Fuller said quickly, 'It isn't anything to do with not being well. Moreen wanted me to call in, since I was passing here today. She saw the hospital people in London – as Doctor Blake arranged. Would you tell him? Also, that her aunt has changed her attitude and Moreen is staying with her.'

Carolyn gave a little cry of thankfulness. Max moved away.

'And Moreen is a little happier?'

'Yes – thanks to all that the Doctor has done. He's seeing to everything connected with the adoption. Nothing can budge her over that... I suppose it's the best thing,' he added a trifle wistfully.

Carolyn understood.

'Funny,' he murmured. 'Now I think of it as my grandchild.' He made a helpless gesture. 'I don't feel any better disposed towards the father, but since he doesn't know the position, there's nothing he can do.'

Carolyn's expression was in the nature of an answer. She saw him to the door and said warmly, 'Please remember me to Moreen. When all this is over–'

'She's not coming back to Lewes,' he interrupted, almost without realising it. 'Wants to stay in London afterwards.'

'She may change her mind about that.'

'I hope so. We all miss her. She is so like

her mother... Thank you, Mrs Blake – for everything.'

Carolyn went back to Max's consulting room. 'Nice man, that.' She might have been talking to herself. 'Nothing in life makes much sense.'

'Is she staying down here?' Max glanced up from some notes he had made on his last patient.'

'No; neither now, nor after the child is born, apparently. Ah, well, let's hope some genuine man comes along to make her happy... Have you the Sinden file?'

He handed it to her. 'Makes happy reading for a change.'

'Yes,' Carolyn said reflectively. 'Reconciliation and now a much wanted pregnancy.'

Max gave a rather hollow laugh. 'Amazing, a doctor's life. Makes nonsense of human relationships.'

They were suddenly aware of the fact that they were alone together. The sudden silence was part of the emotion building up between them. Carolyn broke it by saying quickly, 'If you'll deal with any post now, I can get the letters done – or at least taken down – before you start on your rounds.'

'A good idea.' He did not look at her as he spoke.

She sat facing him across the desk, note pad and pencil ready. He began to dictate slowly, correcting himself far more than usual, and remarking wryly, 'Time I took some lessons. Can't even think straight this morning... And this report, what the hell can I do about it? A massive growth in the cervix which will need therapy to shrink it before anyone can even operate. Ought to have been diagnosed months ago. It isn't always the patients who are wrong. This fellow Pulmar should be given a rocket. Not fit to be in medicine.' Max felt better after the outburst which released some of his own emotional tension. He could not ignore Carolyn and regard her as an efficient machine; he could think only how attractive she was, and how involved he was becoming – the last thing he wished, or had bargained for. 'I'll have to give this report more serious thought. Meanwhile, would you ring and ask the patient to be ready to go into hospital at a moment's notice... Yes, I did warn her of the possibility, and she has suffered so much she is quite resigned; more than that, anxious to get there.'

'Hove, isn't it?'

Max corrected; 'Brighton.'

They finished the letters just as Nigel returned. 'I got there just in time,' he said. 'Coffee?'

The three of them snatched a few minutes break and discussed the patient Nigel had left. 'He's scared, and that doesn't help. Lives a cardiac life and enjoys the excuse for not being able to do half the things he could do. This time he had a blazing row with his wife who is long suffering enough, heaven knows. I got him into hospital. Give them both a rest.'

Carolyn was watching him as he talked, interpreting every shade of expression and intonation of voice. He was speaking quickly, and she felt certain was leading up to some statement which might cause him embarrassment. She was not wrong as, finally, he hastened, 'I have to go over to Hove this afternoon. That patient who was operated on before Christmas.'

Carolyn's thoughts raced – Anita. The patient was a convenient, and doubtless truthful, excuse. 'You mean Edna Hale? But I thought she had made a wonderful recovery after the operation.'

'She had.' His voice was edgy. 'But they've discovered a secondary in the liver.'

'Oh!' Carolyn did not want to pursue the subject. She added, 'I'm sorry... By the way, Mr Fuller called.' She passed on the news about Moreen.

Nigel looked pleased and was grateful for the change of subject. 'I'm glad she is to stay in London when it is all over. In time she will discover how to live and to be happy again.'

Max asked, 'In your experience, Nigel, have you found that adoption turns out to be a blessing for the real mother, or a step she later on regrets?'

'It depends very much on her relationship with the father. Sometimes unhappiness and bitterness bring dislike for the child. Moreen was certainly not bitter – at least to begin with. Her decision about adoption came as a surprise to me. A change of heart I did not expect.' He put down his coffee cup and looked at Carolyn. 'I'll attend to my letters now. I'd like to finish things off here before I go to Hove. May be a bit late back.'

'My picnic with surgery tonight, anyway,' Max said pleasantly. 'The week-end is mine. I've arranged to stay with friends in London. They've just bought, and moved into, a new house at Highgate. You'll have a rest from me.' He grinned, and stood up, his back to the fire. 'This is rather like those last few seconds in bed when one hates to move... A mixed bag today. I reckon I'll be one up on the undertaker by night. I shall be very relieved when I can sign poor old Mrs Whitney's death certificate. There's no magic in old age unless one can enjoy it.'

'And this she did until she fractured her femur,' Nigel remarked. 'At eighty-seven, that's rotten luck. At least she is in hospital and her daughter is having a rest.'

'Better for the daughter when the end

comes, too,' Max said. 'She has been wonderful. Little Mrs Gordon, by the way, seems to think that having twins is a miracle, and with three small children to cope with already–'

Carolyn butted in by asking, 'Why is it you people always talk of *little* Mrs this or that, when you like the patient? And irrespective of their size!'

Max answered, 'We could hardly substitute dear!'

'I suppose,' Nigel remarked, without being the slightest bit interested, 'it is a way of suggesting the patient is someone we respect and admire for their courage... Now to work.'

He dictated to Carolyn for about half-an-hour and just as he was finishing, Freda arrived. She didn't go into any lengthy explanations, but said simply to Carolyn, 'Do you think my doctor could spare me a few minutes – professionally?'

Carolyn's expression became instantly serious. 'Of course. You've caught him – just the right time,' she added to convey the fact that she, Freda, was not causing any inconvenience.

'I ought to have telephoned,' Freda admitted.

Carolyn's trained eye took in her pallor, and the strained, apprehensive look on her usually bright face.

Nigel appeared at the consulting room door.

'A charming patient to see you,' Carolyn said.

'Sorry to worry you at this time,' Freda apologised.

'No question of worrying me... Come in.'

Freda gave a little nervous laugh as she sat down in the patients' chair. 'I came in now because my being out at this time is usual. David has an uncanny instinct, and I was able to tell him that I'd be seeing Carolyn this morning.' She didn't prevaricate as she said, her gaze direct, 'Is it normal to bleed after David has made love to me?'

'No,' Nigel answered, studying her without appearing to do so. 'How long has this been going on?'

'About two months. It isn't long enough to make a fuss about, but I don't like it.' Her voice was anxious. 'I haven't any other symptoms.'

'No intermittent bleeding?'

'On one or two occasions, but I've never been a very regular person, so I didn't take a great deal of notice.'

Nigel nodded. 'Anyway, we'd better see.' He opened the door of the examining room. 'Just call out when you're ready.'

Freda took off the necessary clothing and slipped between the sheets. An electric blanket struck warmly and she relaxed gratefully. It was a relief to be there after going through a period of uncertainty and suspense, even of trying to convince herself that she would be making a fuss to bother Nigel, and that the symptoms would miraculously vanish. She was thankful that coming to Nigel held no embarrassment or uneasiness – only the feeling of safety and security. It was not the first time she'd had a vaginal examination, and was familiar with the procedure.

When it was over Nigel felt the over-whelming relief of being able to say, 'I'd like you to have a few tests, but I think this is a case of a Polypus – very simple to remove.'

'An operation?'

'Very minor.' He smiled.

She said impulsively, 'You're such a comfort. I don't mind much what it is, just as long as I know. One can build up such grim pictures, and I'd hate anything to spoil the kind of life David and I enjoy.'

Nigel looked down at his blotting pad, raised his eyes again, and without realising it said, in a rather flat tone, 'I can understand that... Now how about a coffee? It will give me an excuse for another one... I'll make an appointment at the hospital – purely routine tests.'

'I'd rather not say anything to David until everything is done.'

'That's for you to decide, but I don't agree

with the idea. Would you like him to spare you if the circumstances were reversed? If this were a serious matter one might have second thoughts. As it is, he might imagine that you didn't trust him enough to confide in him.'

'Trust?' Her expression was baffled.

'Because of the nature of the symptom.' He looked at her steadily.

'Oh. I see what you mean. You are right... How quickly can it be done?'

'Within a few days. I'll book you into Manor House.' His laughter was spontaneous, 'Where you had your tonsils removed!'

'That was painful,' she said, making a wry face.

'This won't be. A jab of Pentothal.'

'And oblivion!'

'And forty-eight hours rest,' he said.

Freda grinned. Then became serious. 'Why do I need any tests?'

He didn't hesitate. 'Because I believe in them. The way to avoid an emergency is to prepare for every eventuality. I dislike slovenly medicine just about as much as I dislike slovenly women.' He looked at his watch. 'No time for that coffee.'

Carolyn came out of her room. Nigel was putting on his coat and Freda stood watching him. It was obvious by their attitude that nothing dramatic had happened as the result of Freda's consultation, although Carolyn knew how guarded, even in making a diagnosis, every doctor had to be. He could state the obvious, but not mention the many complications which, while not changing the validity of the original diagnosis, could increase its gravity.

'If I were not a working woman,' Carolyn said glibly, forgetting the implication of the remark, 'I would suggest we had a day off and went into Brighton.' In that second, the thought of Anita and Hove had not entered her mind.

Nigel flashed her a rather challenging look. 'Which goes to prove that one cannot have one's cake and eat it.' He turned to Freda, 'And I can ring you at home at any time?' It was a question that had a double meaning which Freda understood. 'Yes; I shall have a talk to David tonight.'

'Good; now have that coffee and a woman's natter.'

Carolyn asked casually, 'Will you be back for dinner, Nigel?'

'I hope so. It all depends on how things plan out.'

'Then I'll expect you when I see you. Mrs Mortimer will have something for you whatever the time.'

Freda glanced from face to face. They were like two distant friends speaking politely. *Mrs Mortimer will have something for you.* The words sounded foreign, and that was not,

Freda told herself, because she in any way disapproved of Mrs Mortimer being there. On the contrary; it was a matter of Carolyn's dissociation from the household.

The winter sun rifted hazily through the stark trees as Freda and Carolyn stood at the front door and watched Nigel leave. There were patches of blue sky seemingly painted on the backcloth of grey. The air was crisp, and the frost still glistened where the lawn was hidden from the sun.

Carolyn looked questioningly at Freda as the two of them sat over the fire a few minutes later. Freda told her the diagnosis and the relief she felt because she had plucked up courage to see Nigel. 'Oh,' she rushed on, 'not because I minded coming to him, but because I dreaded the thought of having something that might interfere with my life with David. It must be ghastly when that happens to people. Of course it wouldn't change one's love, but... And there's the question of children. When this little job is done, I think I shall have a baby.' As she spoke she noticed the shadow that crossed Carolyn's face and rushed on irrelevantly, 'I thought Max Faber was absolutely charming at the party...' She laughed at herself. 'Although I don't quite know what that has to do with my thinking in terms of having a baby! But seriously, I wasn't wrong about him, was I?'

Carolyn struggled to keep her voice steady. 'No, you were not wrong.'

Freda was almost shocked at the note of seriousness in Carolyn's voice. She could not help saying, 'Caro, you can tell me to mind my own business, but I'd hardly be a friend if I did not sense that you are worried about something.'

Carolyn did not resent the observation, neither did she deny it. 'Just one of those patches,' she said quietly. 'Changes in the practice for instance. I don't know, Freda... I feel rather like the pieces of a jigsaw that don't make a pattern.'

Freda did not make the mistake of narrowing the conversation to an emotional level, although she was anxious about Anita's advent, but reluctant to bring her into the picture in case she projected suspicion into Carolyn's mind.

'I suppose,' she remarked, 'that we all dislike any kind of change and find it takes time to get used to it. When Max gets a place of his own...' She hesitated.

Carolyn felt the colour rise in her cheeks because she knew that she had no desire for Max to leave. His presence was a comfort now that she and Nigel had grown so far apart. Beyond that point she refused to analyse her emotions. Suddenly, and to Freda, disarmingly, Carolyn said, 'I suppose Anita told you that she and Nigel trained at

Princess Ann together? I haven't seen you – at least not in circumstances where I could mention this before. Life is so full of coincidence, and doctors are always meeting old associates.' Carolyn felt that she was speaking parrot fashion.

Freda had not been prepared for the remark and was thankful she could reply with truth, 'No; as a matter of fact she hardly mentioned Nigel. The question of whether, or not, she recalled where she met him – or even if she had met him – did not arise. I suppose so much was going on over the holiday that we hadn't any time really to talk... I was very surprised when she rang me and told me she had joined a practice in Hove... I've seen so little of her during the past few years... Did you like her?'

'I thought she was most attractive.'

Freda noticed the evasion. 'She's changed since the days when I knew her first. Seems much harder. Or, perhaps, that's an unfair remark. I wasn't altogether in the mood for a perpetual party and her vitality exhausted me? She's very clever.'

Carolyn nodded. 'I'm sure she is.'

Freda stayed for about half an hour and had the feeling that Carolyn's thoughts were wandering in all directions. Max came in from his rounds, and Freda could not help noticing that the atmosphere of the house changed; a subtle change which, while bring-

136

ing cheerfulness, also suggested tension.

Max exclaimed with spontaneous delight, 'Twins!' He clicked his fingers. 'As easy as that.'

Carolyn flashed him a smile. 'The "little patient" you spoke of earlier?'

'Yes; I'd called on a routine visit. Thank heaven she wasn't on a bus!'

'You look like a cat that has swallowed the canary!' Freda grinned. 'Must fly, Carolyn.'

'Very attractive girl,' Max exclaimed when Freda had gone. 'I've two patients to see before lunch.'

'Here?'

He nodded.

Mrs Mortimer came into the room at that moment to make certain about the time she should serve the meal.

Carolyn glanced at Max who said, 'I'd be grateful if I could have mine early... Just a snack, so that I do not disturb things.'

'I'll join you.' Carolyn spoke firmly, adding as she addressed Mrs Mortimer, 'It might be a good idea to make the meal late tonight. My husband isn't certain of his plans.'

Mrs Mortimer was not lost to the subtle change that had taken place in the household since the advent of Doctor Faber. 'I can have something ready for you and Dr Faber – something hot – by twelve fifteen. A snack is not very good on a cold day.' She smiled as she spoke.

'Twelve fifteen would be ideal for me,' Max exclaimed appreciatively and looked at Carolyn for her approval.

The matter was settled.

'I'd be very grateful,' Max said, when Mrs Mortimer had gone, 'if you could give me a hand with one of the patients due any minute now. She's sick and tired of doctors. Mother of a younger patient – the Jenkins family – the mother has been appallingly neglected because the husband, son and daughter, have required all the attention. She needs a thorough overhaul and I want smears, cultures – the lot. If you could look after her she'd feel less tense.'

'Anything,' Carolyn agreed gladly. 'It is, after all, my job.' She laughed. 'And while on that subject, it's time I got back to the typewriter. I'll show your patients in.'

'The first appointment, Mrs Jenkins, is the one that matters most. The second is a routine check after a pretty bad enteritis.'

They went to their respective rooms and as Carolyn sat down at her desk the telephone rang. Anita's voice said, 'Oh, Carolyn! Is Nigel there?'

Carolyn felt sudden anger rise. There was such smooth confidence in the question.

'I'm afraid not. Can I give him a message?'

There was a momentary pause before the reply came, 'No; no; it doesn't matter. I'll explain when I see him... Goodbye.' The line went dead and Carolyn replaced the receiver as though dropping something that burned her.

Max, coming into the room, asked, 'Trouble?'

'Not exactly... Ah, your patient,' as the door bell rang at that moment.

Carolyn 'looked after' Mrs Jenkins, settling her on the examining couch and making sure she was comfortable.

'I hate all this,' Mrs Jenkins murmured. 'but I must say Doctor Faber is a man one can talk to, and he put me at ease just now. I hated telling him about my marriage.' She paused and then rushed on, 'I suppose all wives feel the same when they first discover that their husband has another woman. You must hear a great deal of this.'

Carolyn had never heard any words uttered by a patient that struck home quite so hard. She fell back on familiar phrases. 'The great thing is to remember that the average man is terrified of breaking up his home.'

'But not of endangering it.' The words held bitterness. 'If I had the money I'd walk out. Husbands flatter themselves that they are indispensable; it would damage their ego to know how untrue that is.'

Carolyn appreciated that while this woman had talked to Max, she was now giving way to feelings which sprang from outrage and jealousy. Mrs Jenkins gained courage as she spoke. 'I'd like to take statistics on this, and just see how many marriages would remain intact if the woman was financially independent. Cut out duty to the children, and simply go on emotional facts.'

Carolyn did not attempt to comment, knowing that it was enough for Mrs Jenkins to have aired her beliefs.

'It sounds dreadful, Mrs Blake, but quite apart from this – this trouble, my husband bores me until I could scream. Loves the sound of his own voice, knows everything, and listens to nothing anyone else has to say. I suppose the other woman thinks he's clever and amusing. Very different when it's all new, instead of being the same old record played over and over again. I suppose, at heart, I'm sorry for her because he's only a conceited child showing off, and wanting to be centre stage.' She gave a little gasp. 'You must think it dreadful of me to be talking like this, especially when everyone knows how wonderfully happy your marriage is… Anyway it's done me good to let off steam; but I'm sorry for the outburst – and ashamed.' Colour crept into her cheeks. 'Perhaps Doctor Faber can give me something to help. I get so tired, so depressed.'

Carolyn was thankful that Max came in at that moment. She left, not wanting to dwell on what had been said in case it might build up, in her own mind, a situation between herself and Nigel which was an injustice to him. A mood of defiance replaced her former depression, so that when she and Max sat down to lunch together – Nigel not having returned from his rounds and hospital – Max said, 'Am I right in suspecting that you would like to forget all about medicine, doctors, work, and play truant today?'

'Quite right.'

He plunged straight into a subject that was of concern to him. 'I know you said that you would hate to have to face another assistant – someone in my place should things not pan out between Nigel and me – but wouldn't I be correct in saying that you much prefer the house on your own with Nigel? That I am an intrusion in your life.'

They looked at each other and for a second silence fell. Carolyn wished that she could say this was so. Instead, she felt a stirring of emotion, a warmth, which made Max's presence vital to her happiness – if happiness could be defined to represent escape and excitement. Without him now, life would be both empty and bleak. Her voice was very quiet, and each word held significance. 'I prefer your being here; there is no question of intrusion.'

'And I dread the thought of leaving, Carolyn, while knowing that day must come.' His expression was solemn.

They were both acutely aware of each other; of the intimacy of sitting together at the table; even the simple fact of sharing a meal drew them closer. They were hardly conscious of Mrs Mortimer removing their plates, and bringing in the pudding. They ate automatically, eyes meeting eyes in mute appeal for confessions that dare not be made.

And as, later, they drank their coffee in the sitting-room, neither pretended that their relationship could ever be the same again.

9

Anita sat before her dressing table and looked at herself critically in the mirror. She was not conceited, but she was fully aware of her attractiveness. Her skin was fine and creamy, her eyes large, her brows well marked. It was, she decided, an intelligent face, and her even white teeth gave her smile added appeal. Her eyes could have been larger, but their colour more than made up for this fact. Her shining blonde hair, taken up and coiled about the crown of her head, completed a picture she knew to be pleasing. She put the finishing touches to her discreet make-up, and went to her wardrobe in search of the right dress, finally choosing a sheath-like black velvet, which required only her diamond clip and earrings to enhance its simplicity. Nigel had always liked her in black.

The hands of the grandfather clock in the sitting-room appeared not to have moved at all, as she walked towards it from the bedroom. For a second she stood at the large floor to ceiling regency windows and looked out over the gardens of Brunswick Square and down to the sea which shimmered in the fading light of the setting sun. The sky was aflame with colour like some vast furnace spreading its glow over the winter scene, and tinting layers of rifting cloud until they resembled streamers from a maypole.

Three quarters of an hour to wait, Anita thought, before Nigel arrived, always assuming he was not late. He would like this room, with its space and airiness, its shades of gold and soft blues. It had a dignity, and she was proud of her achievement in obtaining the flat and her ability to maintain it. The square was her garden, the trees now like etchings against a flushed darkening sky. For a second the recollection of her call to Lewes disturbed her. She had contrived it at a time when it was likely Nigel would be out, her reason being that she wanted to put herself in the picture. Having met Carolyn, it was far more difficult to adjust herself to the idea that Nigel was married. A shadowy wife could almost be dismissed; the reality meant pain and nostalgia. She began to doubt the wisdom of having brought Freda into the picture in her determination to be invited to Downs Cottage. In fact, she knew that she had played her cards badly, and that not to have telephoned and kept her presence a secret would have been far wiser. Jealousy had urged her to create suspicion in Carolyn's mind.

She tried to shut out any turbulent

thoughts as she drew the curtains and switched on the shaded lamps which made the room glow in a soft welcoming light. The cut glass flashed myriad colours; the decanter with its silver label – a label which Nigel had given her – stood in the centre of the Georgian silver tray.

The door bell rang promptly at five. Her heart felt that it had stopped beating as she hurried to answer it. A strange, almost uncanny sensation overwhelmed her as she opened the door. 'Nigel.' Her utterance of his name was breathless, and a little awed. He looked stern and uncompromising as he took off his coat and followed her into the sitting-room.

'I was lucky to get this flat,' she said in order to break the tension, and because she was far more nervous than she had ever expected to be.

'It is very attractive,' Nigel remarked, 'and the square appeals to me.' He heard himself talking, rather than being involved in what he was saying. His presence there held an element of fantasy, as though he had been transplanted into another world. He noticed the decanter and the silver label; the glasses he had always admired. He noticed also, Anita's dress and admired it. Her taste had always been impeccable.

'It is a little early,' Anita began, 'but won't you have a drink?'

He accepted a whisky gratefully. They raised their respective glasses (Anita's containing sherry), but did not speak. After a second or so he began by asking, 'Why did you have to come here? You told me on Christmas Eve that it was not coincidence, therefore it must have been a deliberate move.'

She did not prevaricate. 'I came because it was the only way I could see you. I'm sorry I spoke about the possibility of having met you before.'

'So am I,' he said gravely. 'And I'm more than sorry you have come into this area.'

Anita put her glass down on the table near her chair. Her eyes focussed him with unnerving intensity. 'We did not part in anger, Nigel.' Her mood was changing in the light of an overwhelming desire.

He lowered his gaze, trying to detach himself from the memories that crowded in.

'I've not forgotten that, either.' His resolution hardened. 'But if you hurt Carolyn in any way whatsoever, I promise that we shall do so. I shall have no mercy on you.'

Her reply was not what he expected.

'The future tense meaning that you do not *wish* to part from me now?'

'Nothing of the kind; it is inevitable that we shall have to meet from time to time, since you are a friend of Freda's. Medical people live in a pretty tightly knit community.' He paused significantly before adding, 'And there is no question of our being involved in any other way.'

'Your visit here hardly substantiates that remark.'

Nigel studied her dispassionately and without self-deception. No one could deny her attractiveness, which amounted to allure. The last thing he had wanted was for the past to catch up with him. He had erased it from his memory as far as was humanly possible. The idea that his own restlessness and sudden dissatisfaction with life had been partly responsible for his agreeing to the meeting, made him uneasy. He had no desire to build up antagonism which could be, in itself, emotion.

'It is better to have an understanding. The last thing I want is for you to see me as the unhappily married man.'

Anita rested her head against the back of her chair and eyed him speculatively. 'And are you happily married?'

'I am in love with my wife,' he answered quietly.

'That does not answer my question,' she said softly.

Nigel knew that what she said was true. He was not unhappily married; he was, at the moment, unhappy. Love, in itself, did not automatically make life simple, or harmonious. 'I do not deny that.' He looked at her steadily. 'Did Max know you were coming here?'

Her surprise was obviously genuine. She shook her head. 'I've not seen Max since I last saw you. I was amazed when I discovered you were associated in the practice.'

'An inevitable arrangement,' Nigel exclaimed regretfully.

'You sound bitter...'

'Not towards him.'

'Then towards me.' Anita lowered her gaze. 'Strange, looking back – a little frightening too. What one is prepared to do for love, and how the years can mock its vows. We were fools, Nigel.'

At that he started. 'Why?'

'We should never have ended things; we should have married.'

'Disenchantment is not the best basis for marriage,' he commented. 'The great thing is to know when to finish a relationship. It is easy to start it. What I want to make absolutely clear is that there can never be any revival of the past, Anita.'

'Are you sure of that?' Her voice was low and enticing.

'Quite sure.' There was a sternness about him that was forbidding. 'I hardly think I need remind you that I am not in your debt in any way.'

She sighed and changed her attitude. 'But I have never needed reminding, and I could never forget all that was done for me.'

Nigel rapped out, 'It is a pity your gratitude did not prevent your coming here.'

She ignored that.

'Carolyn doesn't know anything about me – us?'

'I saw no point in going into it all. There was too much ground to cover. But she knows that she was not the first woman in my life. I did not pretend on that score, and she was not curious.' He added critically, 'If anything were calculated to arouse her suspicions your attitude would have done so. As a matter of fact she did not even mention your name, and while I should have no compunction about telling her the truth, I do not want to rake up the past for no good reason.'

'I was hardly one of many women in your life, Nigel. Neither was our relationship merely a sexual experience.'

'Meaning?'

'That it is harder to accept the existence of one woman, than of several. I doubt if you overlooked that when you generalised about your life to Carolyn. In addition, all that happened would emphasise my importance, and your loyalty.'

'I'm not disputing that; I merely repeat what I came to say.' He studied her, his expression grave. 'You were frank about our meeting on Christmas Eve not being a coincidence. I am being equally frank now. If we are forced to meet in any company, at least we can be pleasant – I hope.'

Anita looked unhappy. She leaned slightly forward as she said, 'I'm still in love with you, Nigel, or I should not have come here.'

'You knew I was married.' He spoke reprovingly.

'True; but I was in your life first, and I have a strange feeling that I shall be in it after Carolyn has gone.'

Nigel gasped, 'Gone... Just what do you mean by that?'

'I come back to my instinct – Max.' Her faint wry smile gave point to her words. 'Ironical.'

'Couldn't it be wishful thinking?' The words came involuntarily. 'Don't force me to believe that you have turned into someone I must despise.'

'I am free to express an opinion – a sincere one, too. I know you well enough to realise that you are certainly not a happy man, despite your protestations. And I most certainly was not looking for any kind of intimacy between your wife and Max.' She paused before adding, 'You will remember my words. They are not spoken maliciously.'

Nigel stared her out before exclaiming, 'Just with intent to implant some poisonous suspicion in my mind.'

Anita was amazed at her own calm. She

felt that she was playing several parts at once, and that the room had become a stage. Nigel's pronouncement did not hurt, or disturb, her. 'On the contrary... And if time proves me wrong, I shall be both surprised and apologetic.' She sighed. 'I still know you quite well; well enough to appreciate that, despite the past, having Max with you is a strain.'

'I could not deny that.'

'He dislikes me,' She spoke petulantly.

'Is there any reason why he should do otherwise? Or have you deluded yourself completely?'

She sighed, her own emotion almost unbearable. 'Oh, Nigel... It seems such a muddle.'

His words rapped out almost fiercely, 'Because you are determined to create one.'

'That's not true.' Her voice broke. 'I behaved badly at your house – I know that. I was jealous, and seeing you again... I don't pretend about my feelings and I cannot wipe out yesterday just because you want me to do so.' She hastened, 'I've been trying to get here – within easy distance of you – since the moment you left London. What do the years matter? I always hoped you'd come back.'

Nigel got up from his chair. 'There is nothing more for us to say, Anita.' He was disarmed by her stillness in that moment.

151

She sat there almost lifelessly, her eyes looking beyond him into space. It reminded him of other days, other hours, when they had been together and some poignant quality about her had, almost against his will, forced upon him decisions both irrational and dangerous.

'Very well.' There was a note of acceptance in her voice and the echo of her words filled the room and lingered in the silence, a silence which cut across Nigel's decision, making him feel ill at ease.

'I did not mean to be hard,' he said.

She moved from her chair and stood beside him. 'I shall be here if ever you need me,' she murmured prophetically.

He made no reply, but flashed her a look of irritation. Not wanting to leave on a note of hostility, he exclaimed, 'You have done well in your profession, Anita. You were always clever.'

'Not,' she corrected meaningly, 'always.'

He stared at her, baffled by the sudden humility. 'We all make mistakes at some time or another.'

When they reached the door and Nigel had put on his overcoat, she lifted her head and lightly touched his cheek with her lips. 'Au revoir,' she whispered.

Nigel went down in the lift to the large square entrance hall, where a wide, magnificent staircase curved to the first-floor flat (testimony of days when one family occupied the entire house) and preserved in the reconstruction of the building to perpetuate a former splendour.

Outside, in the square, the street lights illuminated the stark trees, and the momentary silence was broken only by the sound of the waves beating on the pebbly shore. Nigel stood for a second as though trying to wrest reality out of illusion. He glanced up, sub-consciously, at the bowed, second-floor windows. Anita was looking down on him, one hand holding the curtain aside. She was motionless, and he made no sign. The curtain dropped back into place. He got into his car and drove away, left with the uncanny feeling of having been there before...

10

Nigel returned home that night feeling like an intruder. He cursed himself for not having told Carolyn all the details of his relationship with Anita. Before his marriage it would have been a reasonably straight-forward story; now it had become involved, and his secrecy could not fail to be misconstrued. It was foolish to deny Anita's belief that one love in a man's life was less acceptable to a woman than many. Carolyn could not now fail to take this view, and to make matters worse, Anita was no longer someone in the past; therefore the complic-ations associated with her presence would be far reaching. His theory had always been that detailed confessions were a glorified form of escaping the responsibility for any guilt. Now he was prepared to admit that his silence had been very much bound up with a distaste for acknowledging the depth of his regard for Anita. What, he asked himself, did he feel for her now? No excitement stirred at the thought of her, yet the remem-brances of former happiness lingered a second and then faded into shadow. The sharp edge of anger and violence was lacking, and her attitude had not been antagonistic, or challenging enough, to whip up any real annoyance. His visiting her was an abortive and unnecessary effort; that he had made his point seemed feeble. Nevertheless, he had not brought away with him any feeling of security, or of a problem solved.

Carolyn looked up from the book she was reading as he entered the room. 'Have you eaten?' She spoke as though the question was the most natural in the world, but she knew instinctively that he would not give her any details of his movements, as was his custom.

'I'm not hungry... I'll just have a drink.' He poured himself out a whisky. 'Any calls?'

'From Gillian Conway. Dan was taken ill. Perforated appendix. Max had him rushed to hospital and got hold of James Mace. They should be operating by now.'

'Did Max tell you this?'

Carolyn glanced up and met Nigel's disconcerting gaze. 'No; Gillian telephoned back, wanting reassurance.' Carolyn's mood was defensive. 'Max had enough on his hands without ringing here.'

'I was not suggesting otherwise... Thank heaven he was on call. I'll bet Dan's been suffering a hell of a lot without telling anyone.'

'Yes; Gillian wanted him to send for you earlier. He collapsed.'

'He's always been a stubborn devil; that farm of his is his life. He'll curse the moment he's capable of talking.' Nigel looked anxious. He and Dan were good friends. 'Max was lucky to get hold of James Mace.'

'Apparently he tracked him down at his club.' And all the time she was talking Carolyn was thinking of Anita, and how obvious it was that Nigel had been to see her. In different circumstances he would have expressed regret because he had not been at home to attend to Dan, who was an old patient of his. Also there was something alien about him, rather like a man who had suddenly changed into an ill-fitting suit in which he was uncomfortable. She said deliberately, 'I tried to contact you, but you had left the hospital.'

Nigel poured himself out a second drink. He made no comment on Carolyn's statement. It must be obvious to her that he had not come straight home, and since he could not tell her the truth, silence was the best policy.

'I think I'll get over to Lewes,' he said suddenly, putting the glass down without drinking the whisky.

'Gillian's at the hospital. She went in the ambulance with Dan.'

'She might like to come back here for the night.'

'I suggested it, but there are the animals to

look after.'

Nigel nodded. 'In that case I can run her back to the farm...' He hesitated as though about to add something and thought better of it.

'She would appreciate that. After all, Max is a stranger to her... How did you find your hospital patient?'

'She's being operated on again in a couple of days. Miracles sometimes happen,' he added.

Carolyn got up from her chair. She stood slim and aloof. Nigel noticed that she had been to the hairdresser, and that she was wearing a new dress of velvet, the shade of rich claret. He could not recall her having worn velvet before, and the fact sent a curious sensation over him as though she and Anita were like interwoven threads in a tapestry – the tapestry of his life. He could not bring himself to comment on her appearance, and felt a stab of jealousy. Was this for Max's benefit?

Carolyn tried not to allow her emotions to become unruly as, once again, she watched him drag on his overcoat. It seemed symbolic of their life which had become a perpetual monotony.

Mrs Mortimer appeared as the front door shut.

'Oh dear,' she said, 'doctor had to go out again?'

Carolyn forced a laugh. 'Every doctor's house should have a bed and breakfast sign. No extra charge for night calls,' she added facetiously. 'I think I'd love another coffee, Mrs Mortimer.'

It was brought as quickly as possible. 'And now you go to bed,' Carolyn insisted. 'Whatever may be needed I can get... No argument.'

'There's cold chicken in the larder and freshly made soup in a container in the fridge. It seems bitterly cold to me. Freezing hard outside. Probably more snow on the way – just to make things more awkward. Good night.'

Carolyn tried to read again. The sentences became meaningless and concentration impossible. After an hour of wandering aimlessly, of switching on the wireless and television, and turning them both off in turn, she decided that she would make a cup of tea. She had drunk enough coffee for one evening. The kitchen gleamed brightly, the sink units polished, every utensil shining almost like silver. Having plugged the kettle in, she realised she could not possibly drink tea, anyway. And, at that moment, she heard a car drive into the garage and a tremor went over her as she realised that it was Max.

He came into the house, met her gaze, and said, 'Mace did a magnificent job... Nigel has taken Mrs Conway back to the farm.

I'm glad he was able to get to the hospital.'

Carolyn automatically, and instinctively, poured him out a whisky.

'Thanks.' He flopped down in a chair.

Carolyn said, 'I always swear I will not get involved with the ills of patients and friends, but I always do. In my next life I shall marry some nice, comfortable agricultural family.'

'And worry about the lambs being born when the weather is foul.'

Carolyn smiled. 'I know! And when they are dug out of the snow.'

He looked at her across the few feet that separated them, holding her gaze deliberately. 'You realise that I shall be away for New Year's Eve?'

'Yes.'

'I chose the week-end deliberately. I did not want to be here.'

'Oh.' Her voice dropped.

'I'm sure David and Freda's party at the Bedford will be a marvellous affair and that I'd be very welcome, but–'

Carolyn admitted, 'I am not enthusiastic. The days seem rather odd, in fact. But as Freda goes into the nursing home early in the New Year...' She stopped, realising that she was not making sense. 'I'm sorry you are not coming with us.' As she paused she lowered her gaze. 'What will you be doing... I mean, how are you going to celebrate?'

'Visiting one or two friends. Nothing

much. What I want to do is another matter... Do you like dancing?'

'Love it.'

'And Nigel?'

'He's fond of it too, but we haven't been to a dance for ages. I don't really know why...'

'There is something rather special about dancing the New Year in with the right person,' Max said significantly. 'By the way, I think that – subject to agreement – I have found a cottage near Beddingham. Furnished, and with one vital thing – a telephone.'

Carolyn felt suddenly breathless; her expression was startled. 'Very sudden... I mean–' She floundered.

'A matter of caution, not of desire, Carolyn.'

Their respective thoughts seemed visual, as though the pattern of their lives lay starkly in the little gulf of space which separated them physically.

'Have you been over it?'

'Yes. It is well furnished and owned by a man who has gone to America and wants a six months let. His daily is part of the rent, so that she can keep the place as he likes it.' Max paused. 'I realise that I cannot go on living here.'

Colour touched Carolyn's cheeks. A wave of excitement flowed over her because there was no mistaking his meaning. Had he said,

'I love you,' he could not have conveyed his feelings more explicitly. The tone of his voice, his expression, the way he looked at her – all built up to a crescendo of emotion. She did not comment; there were no words with which rightly to explain her feelings.

'Obviously,' he went on, 'I shall have to use Downs Cottage as my professional base until I am finally settled and have a permanent home. I shall have to discuss this with Nigel, but I wanted to explain to you first.'

'Thank you; I appreciate your confidence.' The house already seemed lonely at the thought of his leaving. She introduced a lighter note, 'You will still need to have your letters typed, and the files kept in order. Doctors are hopelessly untidy and unorganised without a secretary around.' She wondered, suddenly, and with a pang, if this was his first move towards severing his association with Nigel, and finding another practice.

He read her thoughts. 'I want to remain working here. I hope nothing happens to prevent it. Nigel is a very fair man,' he added spontaneously, 'and doesn't try to do my job as well as his own. He is also a very fine doctor – as you well know.'

Carolyn knew and nodded her assent. She had the curious feeling that she was talking about a stranger. There were many things she would have liked to ask Max about the past, and why it was necessary for so much secrecy, but loyalty to Nigel forbade it. In turn Max wished that he could confide in her; not merely about Nigel, but his own personal problems that had nothing to do with medicine, or his ambitions in that direction. He disliked the fact that he was hiding a vital truth from them both which, should he divulge it, might result in the severance of any association, and change their whole attitude towards him. He recognised his own weakness, and despite his resolution to make amends, could not endure the possibility of losing Carolyn's regard and respect. He hurried over the thought of the word *regard*, because he had come to believe that her feelings for him were far deeper than she would ever admit.

'It is ironical that I wanted to be near Lewes,' he said abruptly. 'Quite apart from any professional ambitions.' He stopped, hesitating before adding perkily, 'I wanted to look up someone I'd known rather well...'

Carolyn was startled. She sensed his words were in the nature of a confession. 'Someone who comes into the category of your regrets?'

'Why do you say that?'

'I honestly do not know.'

'You are right all the same.' He sounded relieved.

'What happens,' Carolyn asked sadly, and in the voice of one talking to herself, 'to our loves? Nothingness, after so much ecstasy. Yet we go on hopefully to another experience, repeating our emotional follies and mistakes.'

'This was not a love,' he explained honestly, 'it was an episode, if you like, without any thought of permanency.'

'On both sides?' Carolyn's gaze was steady and a little perplexed.

'As far as I understood; but responsibility catches up with one.'

'At least it shows maturity to accept it.' She felt a strange presentiment in that second, not wanting to hear anything that might cut across their present harmony. Nevertheless she recalled their conversation on Christmas Eve, and his frankness about his life. 'Why,' she asked, 'are you talking to me like this now?'

'I don't think I could give you a truthful answer to that question, unless it is because I do not want you to have any illusions about me, and because, too, my outlook has changed. Perhaps discovering a capacity for loving makes one appreciate the hurt one has inflicted in the past, and the enormity of one's selfishness. Rather like seeing a true picture of oneself for the first time. Not a pleasant experience. I can't run away any more, Carolyn.' He added almost gravely,

'That is why I am going to London – in the hope of making some kind of peace with my conscience.'

'I see.' She met his gaze.

'How much would you forgive a man?'

She did not hesitate. 'Everything if he told me the truth. If he gave me credit for understanding that emotion sways, exults and distorts to such an extent that most acts appear to be permissible at the *time*. No story, told in retrospect, captures the day to day events; the gradual building up of tension; the conflicts. It always seems as though two people had deliberately, and wantonly, plunged into chaos at a single given moment, without any crescendo of feeling.'

'God, how true that is,' he said fervently. 'Like a case reported in the newspapers.'

They were silent for a few seconds. The sound of Nigel's car made Max say quietly, 'I'm glad I've talked to you. Thank you for listening, for helping.'

'I cannot see in what way I've helped.' As she spoke, Carolyn was conscious of his presence almost as a challenge. Her body heated at the thought that she might have misunderstood the eloquence of his restraint during the past few days. The words rushed out, 'Will – I mean – are your plans likely to change in view of all this?'

'Certain not during this probation period...'

'This,' hastened Carolyn, 'has been a very sudden decision.'

'Yes.' He held her gaze intently. 'As far as loyalty permits, I shall tell you my plans when I get back.'

Nigel joined them. He looked exhausted. 'You did a good job, Max. Getting Mace was excellent.'

'Thanks.' Max smiled. 'It may be corny, but it is still true that appendicitis can be the graveyard of surgeons.'

Nigel sat down and lay back in his chair. Carolyn got him a drink and asked, as she handed it to him, 'Would you like anything to eat?'

'Nothing thanks.' He took the glass thankfully. He was cold and dispirited. The moment work stopped his own problems crept back. He glanced at Max then at Carolyn. What had they been discussing in his absence? Although they were relaxed in each other's company, they nevertheless radiated a certain excitement. Or was that his imagination feeding upon Anita's suspicions?

Max left them alone and within a few minutes of the door closing, Carolyn said quietly, 'I'm going up; it's late... A worrying time,' she added. 'I'm thankful everything is all right so far.'

Nigel finished his drink and got up from his chair. 'I'm ready for bed,' he said and stopped as though the word embarrassed him.

Carolyn hurried ahead, leaving him to turn off the lights.

Nigel waited tensed for her to ask him about his visit to Hove, but no mention was made of it. It struck him painfully that when a wife ceased to ask questions, or to be concerned about her husband's movements, it could be one of two things; wisdom or indifference, and in Carolyn's case he felt sure it was the latter...

11

Max found himself in London and seemed to have reached there in a trance. He knew that he might be jeopardising everything he valued, but was urged on by a force stronger than anything he had ever known before. The journey from Lewes might have taken place in another life, yet the atmosphere which saturated the downland countryside, seeped into him, increasing the poignancy and depths of his own turbulent thoughts. He hated every second that took him away from Carolyn, and he no longer hid the truth of his feelings, accepting them with an inevitability which, at the moment, filled him with emotion both new and frightening.

On his arrival at Victoria he hired a taxi to Markham Street, which was just behind Marble Arch. A quiet, old-fashioned street, reminding him of gas lamps and very stuffy drawing-rooms; of houses where once the staff had worn black, with white frilly aprons and caps. Now every building had been converted into flats, creating an anonymity that was part of modern life. Almost guiltily he refreshed his memory from the address he had taken down from a case file in Nigel's cabinet. He paid the taxi driver, mounted the few steps, and pressed a bell beside the name Cole. In a few seconds the door was opened and Moreen Fuller greeted him with a gasp of surprise and amazement which held no welcome.

'I must talk to you,' Max said directly.

'There's nothing to talk about,' she replied emphatically, and was on the point of shutting the door.

Max put out a hand and widened the space so that he could step into the corridor. It struck him that, despite her pregnancy, she had retained an untouched beauty which smote him.

'All I ask is a chance to explain,' he said.

She closed the door and looked up at him. 'Rather late for that, isn't it?' Her voice held no anger, no bitterness; her comment was purely factual.

'Perhaps; but not too late... Are you alone?'

'Yes; they are out shopping. They won't be back for an hour.' She led the way into a small, but well furnished, sitting-room and switched off the television which was turned down very low. No emotion showed in her expression, and her acceptance of his presence – after the first reaction of fear – was unnerving.

'I'm sorry,' he began, 'I haven't come before.'

She looked at him speculatively. 'At first I prayed you would come. Seeing you at Downs Cottage was such a shock that I hated you. Hated the lies you told me.' Her glance lowered to her ringless hands, 'But you can resign yourself to anything if you try hard enough.'

She looked so young and, contradictorily, so strong and resolved, that her words might have been uttered by a woman three times her age.

'You must still hate me,' he said with a painful regret.

She shook her head. 'No; I still love you, but it is almost faraway.'

'Love,' he echoed, shocked.

'I suppose I didn't realise until afterwards. I shouldn't have done as I did – not really – unless I'd loved you; but we don't always know love when we find it.'

Her words struck home.

'No,' he repeated, 'we don't always know, or perhaps recognise, love when we find it. I'm sorry I lied to you.'

'So am I,' she said phlegmatically, 'it destroyed something that I valued and, at the same time, did me a good turn.'

'Good heavens, how?'

'Made my decision for me. After that, I didn't want to keep the baby. Before, I'd built up a romantic story around it, seen myself as suffering for love – almost as a heroine for not telling them who the father was. I suppose all girls go mad when they first discover they're pregnant. I was terrified, and I dreaded hurting my father... Didn't it occur to you that I might have a baby?'

'Yes; and that was one of the reasons why I was anxious to work near Lewes. Not, I admit, the most important one – to my shame – but I intended to come to see you and then when you arrived at Downs Cottage...' He paused, lost for words.

'You don't have to explain. You were scared stiff of the truth leaking out and when you knew – and I'm sure they told you – that the baby was to be adopted, you felt relieved because it seemed to let you out.' She stared at him. 'All men are moral cowards. I've learned a lot in these past months.'

Max could not deny the piercing truth of her words. It was the first time in his life that he felt completely inadequate. There was nothing he could say that would match her simple, yet damning truths, and the fact that she spoke so quietly, without rancour, added ten-fold to his self indictment.

'And you can still say you love me?' His amazement was obvious. 'I should have thought you'd loathe the sight of me.'

'I'll never forget seeing you before I fainted... Love seems an awful mixture of love and hate. And then, when my aunt was kind and I found a home here – not just for charity's sake – I suppose I saw things in a different light. You didn't tell me you loved me, or talked of doing so. You just made sure that you could not be dragged into marriage. America, and an engagement, tied all the loose ends up.'

'It sounds damnable,' he said in self disgust.

'Truth does – half the time.' She added swiftly, 'You've changed, Max.'

The sound of his name on her lips sent a tremor over him.

'Not before I needed to do so... Moreen, I haven't told you why I'm really here. Will you marry me? We could–'

She interrupted him. 'Do you love me?'

'Not in the sense you mean,' he admitted honestly.

'I don't want to marry your conscience,' she said quietly. 'And I don't agree with marrying for the wrong reason.'

'But the child?'

'We took the risk of having it.' Her voice was full of conviction. 'And the risk of a broken home later on would double the wrong.'

'But,' he protested, 'you cannot possibly assume there would be a broken home.'

'I can reject the possibility of one. Doctor Blake has a wonderful couple for the baby to go to – a lovely home where it will be happy and loved. The longer I think about it, the more grateful I am.'

'And you?' His voice was uneven, his eyes dark and troubled.

'I try not to think of myself. It all seems strange and unreal, as though it will never be born.'

The baby... His child. Max felt that all the blood in his veins had heated to an abnormal temperature. He was brought up against the stark fact that there was no right on his side. Although Moreen was very mature for her age, she had still been only eighteen when he made love to her. Her youth, her spontaneous gaiety, her capacity for giving, had blinded him to the enormity of his offence. Now, sitting there, the repercussions stunned him, and her loyalty became almost unbearable.

'What made you protect my name?'

'At first my love for you, and after I discovered that you were with Doctor Blake... Well, you see, it would only have hurt him, and not done any good. If you'd wanted to come to me—' Her voice broke for the first time.

'Listen,' Max said urgently, 'Moreen, you must listen. If you can possibly forgive me, don't you realise that I can look after you? That we can see this thing through together.'

'I'm too young to marry without being loved.' Her eyes rounded appealingly. 'As for forgiving you – that doesn't come into it.

I think it's a silly word – forgiving. I can't hold it against you because you are not in love with me. Marriage would probably wreck both our lives. I'm young enough to love again. I want to *be* loved, too. Now, to be your wife would be such an easy way out, but if I took it I'd be a coward. And perhaps when we were really married I'd discover that I didn't love you after all, and that it was emotion because of the baby.' She added, 'But I'm glad you came, it takes away the – the abandoned feeling. Gives me back my memories, too. I've missed those.'

'Oh Moreen,' he murmured hoarsely.

She felt suddenly very lonely. It was an upsurge of emotion both painful and nostalgic. Strange, to the point of disbelief, that she had slept in this man's arms, been awakened by him to the ecstasy of sex, with all its sensuality, tenderness, and loving. It was like returning to explore a once familiar world that was now forbidden. She knew the way he dressed and undressed; the way he slept; his habits, and she could feel his fingers threading through her long hair and then caressing her face. His attractiveness was a power, and she could not fault his treatment during the time they were together. It could have been written as an idyll. To her it had been all truth; to him a fact built upon a foundation of convenient lies, told to prevent her taking him seriously so far as any future was concerned. She wondered how many other women had shared a similar experience with him. She did not regret her lost virginity, because it would seem like cheating the desire that had been responsible for it. It had, she knew, made her mature far beyond her years, just as she had always seemed older than those in her own age group.

'You will hear about me through Doctor Blake,' she said a little breathlessly, 'and I shall stay with my father from time to time, when all this is over. You won't know anything about the baby, any more than I shall, and I shan't ever see it.' Her eyes were suspiciously bright. 'I wouldn't like to wreck its life for the sake of a few minutes.'

Max found he could not speak. How many times had he listened to cases like this. The heartache, the tragedy, and the final renunciation. How many men had he condemned with contemptuous disgust. He burst out, 'I must help because I want to; don't deny me that. Or misunderstand it.'

She hesitated before saying, with childish simplicity, 'I'd like some flowers. Not with any card with them...' Her voice faltered. She got up and went to a writing desk in the corner, taking an envelope from it. 'If you address this to yourself I can let you know when it's over. My writing would be recognised,' she added in explanation. 'I shall just put a note inside, giving you the date, and the ward.'

Max did as she asked, and she took the envelope from him and put it in her handbag. Her face was suddenly composed and serene.

'I want your promise that if you should change your mind about me you will let me know,' he said gently and urgently.

She shook her head. 'That way we should neither of us be free.' Her gaze darted to the clock. 'And now you must go so that I can rest before they get back.'

'I haven't explained half that I came to explain, told you–'

She stopped him. 'You came – that was important.'

'I think it would have been easier if you had treated me as I deserve to be treated,' he said vehemently.

She gave him a little smile which seemed as if all the wisdom of time had inspired it.

His last glimpse of her was as he reached the bottom of the steps and looked back from the pavement before she closed the door...

12

Nigel dressed for the New Year's Eve Ball at the speed of a hurricane. Since Max was away, Mrs Mortimer had his telephone number at the hotel in case of emergency. He told himself that, since the day had been full of them, by the law of averages he might reasonably expect a respite. Casualty wards would be crowded with the debris of crazy motorists, and he thanked heaven that he was spared the spectacle, plus the frantic fight to save life.

'Is this going to be a large party, or just the four of us?' He was endeavouring to manipulate his bow tie as he spoke.

Carolyn walked across the bedroom to where he was standing before the long panel mirror. She was wearing a shimmering white dress, embroidered with a delicate silver thread. 'Let me,' she said smoothly and began, expertly, to complete the job at which he always failed.

Nigel was aware of her nearness and of the subtle perfume that enveloped her. Every sense was electrified by her presence, and he realised that he was living every moment on the razor edge of emotion.

Carolyn was thinking of Max and was lost to her surroundings.

'Party,' she echoed vaguely. 'I really don't know who is coming. I assume that Anita will be there.' Her voice was controlled. Just then it really did not matter about Anita. 'How long will Freda be in the nursing home?' The change of subject left Nigel no opening for discussion that might involve Anita.

'After the tests, a couple of days – all being well... That is a very lovely dress, and the scarlet coat over it – perfect. I wonder what Max will be doing tonight.' Nigel gave a little forced laugh. 'Having a real bachelor celebration.'

Carolyn felt a pang of jealousy. 'The house seems strange without him,' she said deliberately.

'You know about the cottage near Beddingham?' Nigel looked at her quizzically.

'Yes; he did mention it. Sounds ideal.'

'I thought it rather odd suddenly to take a place like that.'

'I don't see why.' Carolyn picked up her bag and gloves. There was a defensive note in her voice.

'Must have got fed up with living here.'

'Perhaps.'

'I rather think that he has some personal reason for making two moves where one would do.' Nigel continued talking as they went down the stairs. 'It wouldn't surprise me if he suddenly got married.' The remark was made deliberately as he watched for any change of expression on Carolyn's face.

In that split second, Carolyn was taken off her guard. 'What,' she asked breathlessly, 'makes you say that?'

'Call it a man's intuition, with suspicion thrown in.'

Carolyn could not deny that the possibility hurt her; that it crystallised her views and touched the heart of her fears. Max had told her a great deal – and nothing before he left for London. His question, 'How much would you forgive a man?' might well have been linked with his own affairs and his remark, 'This was not love' could nevertheless involve great depth of feeling. She said a little tersely, 'The word suspicion is hardly applicable. Max is a single man and free to do precisely what he chooses.'

Nigel felt that a heavy weight was crushing his heart. Carolyn's attitude made her reactions so obvious.

'Freedom of choice is not always the prerogative of the single...You are very fond of Max.' The words rushed out, emotion tearing at him.

'Yes,' she admitted freely, 'he is a person easy to miss.'

'I must go away for a week-end,' Nigel said a little savagely.

She flashed him a cynical smile. 'You never appear to be here in any case.'

Her tone angered him, touching the raw spot of guilt. 'I must learn to make pretty speeches,' he retorted pointedly.

They went out to the car and, as they did so, a figure reached the front door.

'Max!' Carolyn spoke in a breath.

Nigel's annoyance increased. 'What on earth are you doing – back so soon?'

Max was looking at Carolyn, the light from the porch lamp illuminated her face, revealing the beauty of the shimmering ensemble she was wearing.

'Such a welcome,' Max remarked.

'Are you joining us later on?' Nigel asked.

'No; no thank you. I just got fed up with London. I'll keep the medical fort,' he added, 'and patch up any little dears who happen to bash their heads in tonight... Enjoy yourselves.'

Carolyn could not overcome the upsurge of excitement, followed by the suspense of wondering, and fearing, what might have happened. 'Nigel has been saying that it wouldn't surprise him if you suddenly got married.'

It was Max's turn to be both startled and uneasy. 'Why on earth should you think that?' He addressed Nigel.

'Am I right?' Nigel's gaze was challenging.

'No; entirely wrong.' He tried to avoid

Carolyn's gaze, but their eyes met and emotion surged between them. 'My remembrances to everyone,' he added, as he stood beside the half-open window on Carolyn's side of the car. 'I'll toast you all at midnight, and wish you both a happy New Year in advance. I shall take a book and a drink to bed with me.'

Nigel's voice was almost harsh as he exclaimed, 'Which sounds like my idea of heaven.' He thrust the engine into gear and the car shot forward jerkily.

Carolyn said, just before they reached the gate, 'There is nothing to stop you from following Max's example. I'm quite capable of driving into Hove.'

'Don't be absurd. I just feel tired.'

'You should see a doctor,' Carolyn flashed back facetiously. 'You are always tired. It certainly hasn't been through lack of sleep since Max has worked in the practice.'

Her words stung; he had no answer because he was afraid to get involved in any emotional discussion. Jealousy undermined his control; he could not think rationally, or employ any tact.

'My sleeping habits seem to offend you,' he said accusingly, suspicion prompting the remark. 'You could hardly know how well I sleep unless you were awake yourself. I'd hate to be the cause of your insomnia. Or is it that you regard sleep as a crime instead of a normal function?' He finished bitterly, 'perhaps it would be better if we occupied separate rooms.'

Carolyn's hands clenched in her lap. The guilt of her stupidity increased her resentment. 'I think separate rooms would be an excellent arrangement.'

There was a tense, almost electric, silence before Nigel said grimly, 'Then that's settled.'

A bleak, forlorn sensation touched Carolyn as anger died. She realised then why it was so much easier to settle differences after a fierce, violent quarrel. Emotion, thus aroused, could swing from rage to passion, and end on the exquisite note of both mental and physical reconciliation. This cold, almost clinical, disunity destroyed even the essence of compromise, leaving only the emptiness of an ever widening gulf.

13

Anita took one look at Nigel as he and Carolyn entered the hotel that night, and made their way to David and Freda who stood awaiting them. She knew of old his tight-lipped expression; the slight backward tilt of his head, and the glint of steel in his eyes. Carolyn, too, was obviously assuming an air of happy anticipation which she was far from feeling.

'Where's Max?' Freda's voice held a note of disappointment.

Nigel explained, finishing with, 'But he returned just as we were leaving and sent his New Year wishes.'

Carolyn glanced around her at the attractively dressed women and the men looking their best in dinner jackets. On the surface it all appeared highly successful – the beginning of a gay evening to bring in another year. The smiles, the flirtatious glances, the adoring ones; and the mask-like expressions on the faces of those who were either at the wrong gathering, or with the wrong partner. She was conscious of Anita's steady gaze and half questioning attitude as she said, 'Carolyn, you do not look too well … or is that a dreadful *faux pas* on the part of a doctor?' She laughed. 'We are not supposed to notice anything that isn't brought to our attention.'

Carolyn forced a laugh. Perhaps Nigel's earlier behaviour was intended to be deceptive because, in truth, he was excited by the prospect of Anita being at the party. The prospect. Of course, he would have known in advance. The telephone was a permanent form of communication.

'I'm perfectly well, I assure you; perhaps my make-up is all wrong.'

'Nonsense,' David insisted. 'It's perfect.' He was annoyed by Anita's presence, but when she had telephoned to suggest a party for New Year's Eve, there was little they could do except include her in their plans. When the question of an escort arose, she was emphatic that she much preferred to come on her own. Nevertheless, Freda made it her business to invite a friend of David's, Richard Maitland, a solicitor with a practice in Brighton. He arrived at that moment. He was tall, fair and extremely good looking. Anita flashed Freda a faintly critical glance. It was obvious that he was to be her partner. When he was introduced she merely inclined her head, her eyes cold and distant.

Carolyn was thankful for the first drink. She felt that every word was an effort, and that she was incapable of conversation, until

David, eyeing her as she began her second drink, said softly, 'You'll feel better after that.'

'Is it,' Carolyn whispered, 'so noticeable?'

'To me, yes. What's wrong?'

'I don't quite know... Anyway, you're looking very attractive and Freda's in good form.' They exchanged glances which, while endeavouring to conceal concern, had the reverse effect. 'She'll be fine, David. Nothing to worry about – honestly.'

'I know; that's what so stupid; it doesn't prevent my feeling quite sick at the thought of it all. Thank God for Nigel.'

Carolyn nodded agreement. No one thought more highly of him than she when it came to his profession. The element of unreality increased. Separate rooms. What had happened to the two people who had once been so happy together? They sat there now, meeting each other's gaze with veiled hostility, talking in a clipped, faintly bitter tone when it was necessary for them to address each other. Anita had managed to sit next to him as they drank their cocktails. It had been a subtle manoeuvre which had forestalled Freda's intention of making certain that she and Richard were together. There was something blatantly obvious in Anita's attitude towards Nigel; an attitude which conveyed an intimacy, both in manner and speech, possible only between those whose relationship had been completely outside the realm of friendship. He looked ill at ease as she insinuated little references to the past on the lines of 'Do you remember?' Carolyn ignored them. She had reached the dangerous stage when she had no intention of taking up the challenge.

The gloom lifted by the time the dinner table had been reached. It was an excellent meal, and the decorations were both attractive and artistic. The guests were gay without being rowdy. When the lights went down at midnight Carolyn sat tensed as she waited for Nigel's greeting; when it came he lifted her hand and kissed it; their eyes met across what seemed to be a desolate waste. No emotion stirred in her, not even when she watched him greet Anita in precisely the same way. Later, after the Cabaret, she wished she could avoid having the first dance of the New Year with him, but that was not possible. As they followed David and Freda on to the floor (Anita forced to have Richard for her partner), Nigel said, 'I wonder what we shall be doing next year?'

'Not having a crystal ball I cannot make any prediction,' she replied with polite calm. 'The mystery of tomorrow is a perpetual suspense story. Perhaps that is why we bear our respective lives.'

'We all have the power to change them.'

Was that his way of suggesting that he

wished to change his, or that she was free to change hers?

She glanced up at him. 'Some people manage to have their cake and eat it. Both clever and simple... Quite amusing to look around here tonight and wonder what would happen if truth tore off the masks.'

'I doubt if even *you* could apply that to David and Freda.' He spoke with reproach.

Carolyn's expression softened; her voice became gentle. 'No; they stand for everything I admire. They're so happy.'

Nigel stiffened. Previously that remark had always applied to themselves.

Carolyn felt the tug of remembrance, realising that words, far from being an ally, could be an enemy. Once understanding and communication had gone, everything became a distortion.

Nigel experienced a certain defiance as he danced with Anita a little later. Her supple body touched his, and he could feel the heavy thudding of her heart like a pulse between them.

'This is heaven,' she whispered, her eyes starry.

'You are behaving very badly,' he said angrily. 'That possessive air – it must stop, Anita.'

'I was not aware of behaving like that.' She looked innocent. 'I suppose it is second nature. I cannot feel strange with you... I cannot pretend to myself that I've never lain in your arms, or been loved by you. I feel rather like a first wife who has a prior claim.'

'That is utterly absurd. Suppose all women adopted such an attitude?'

'You do not dislike it half as much as you pretend, Nigel.' Her voice was caressing, her hand tightened its grip on his. 'You are a very lonely man. Love can bring emptiness as well as ecstasy. You refuse to believe what your heart knows is true. Max is far more Carolyn's type than you are.' She paused significantly. 'I should say she is just as starved of emotion as you. I feel very wise when I see you both floundering, not really knowing in which direction you are going.'

It was impossible for Nigel to sustain his cold, withdrawn attitude. The atmosphere, the music from a Latin American band, stirred his senses, bringing a reluctant awareness of Anita's vibrant charm and her unmistakable desire for him. For a few brief moments he relaxed, shutting out the problems, feeling alive again. And then he looked straight into Carolyn's eyes across the ballroom as she danced with Richard Maitland. It was like coming face to face with a stranger.

Anita did not play up her advantage, and they finished the dance in silence. She murmured, as they walked back to the table, 'Thank you for giving me a few moments of

… yesterday.'

Just before the party broke up, Anita said, 'And now it is my turn to give a party. Freda, when you are back in circulation again, will you and David come over to my flat for a quiet little dinner?'

Freda was reluctant to accept, but had no alternative. Carolyn realised that to refuse, when Anita asked if she and Nigel would join them, would make the matter an issue. Richard was included and, as it was at some unspecified time, accepted.

'I'll give you plenty of warning,' she promised.

Richard felt that a year would be too short. There was something predatory about Doctor Benson that he both disliked and suspected. She was the last person he could imagine Freda having for a friend.

It was two o'clock before they finally parted and went to their respective cars. The moon spilled molten gold upon a calm sea, and the night was still and full of promise, as though identified with the beginning of a New Year. Nigel and Carolyn were silent on the journey back, apart from a few stilted observations about the evening. When they reached the house, there was only one thought uppermost, and Nigel voiced it as he said, 'I'll sleep in the dressing room. I take it the bed is made up as usual?'

Carolyn tried to sound calm. 'Yes.'

It was a room originally designed for the first offspring. It communicated with the main room, and there was access to the bathroom from a door on the landing. On rare occasions Carolyn had slept in it when having a heavy cold and not wishing to disturb Nigel's sleep. It had always been a joke because, after one night alone, Nigel invariably lured her back, but the bed was always in readiness for any emergency.

They stood in the sitting room which suddenly had a bare, empty look as though denuded of furniture. Nigel poured himself out a brandy, champagne having left him completely sober – painfully so. He watched Carolyn covertly, wondering if she would make any comment, or elaborate on anything previously said. The silence was uncanny and wounding, because it emphasised the truth that they had nothing to say to each other – neither recrimination, nor explanation. He had no idea how to begin to talk to her, and every moment that ticked away widened the gulf between them. He wished he happened to be the type who could use desire and passion to plead his cause; the type to whom words came glibly, easily. It was like standing and watching some sacred part of himself destroyed. Carolyn's silence about Anita was far more shattering than accusation. No wife could possibly fail to have noticed Anita's possessiveness that night. Nigel would have welcomed jealousy, whereas this cool acceptance could only mean an indifference born of a new love – Max. Anita was undoubtedly right he thought; women were intuitive about these things.

Suddenly they were alerted by the sound of a key turning in the front door lock, and as they both hurried to the hall, Max came into the house.

Max said rather wearily, 'I'm the bright boy with an idea of bed, a book, and a drink! Instead, I've been looking after a friend of Martin Cook. Aneurism – arch of the aorta – with angina thrown in for good measure. Poor devil. The hospital will love me tonight.' Max took off his coat and the three of them went into the sitting-room together.

Nigel, trying to talk naturally, said, 'The Cooks always get this sort of thing. I take it the patient was staying with them?'

'Yes.'

'I remember they had friends with them last Easter and the wife went into labour three weeks ahead of time. I delivered the baby and Miriam Cook did the nursing!' Nigel was thankful for the opportunity of talking work.

Carolyn was conscious of Nigel's watchful eyes, and could not endure the tense atmosphere. She went up to bed, put Nigel's pyjamas into the dressing-room, used the bathroom as quickly as possible, and left the door which led to the landing ajar. Looking round her as she sat at her dressing table, removing her make-up, it seemed that the room was twice its normal size, and filled with a silence almost as deep as that which accompanied death. Death of a marriage. There was an ache within her which was as unbearable as a physical ailment; but it was an ache that had not come suddenly, and had slowly increased with time. These were not circumstances where she could slip back into Nigel's arms in an act of simple reconciliation. They had been just as far apart while sleeping in the same bed, as they would be tonight sleeping in separate rooms. The difference was that, until now, the façade of marriage had been preserved. The thought of Max cut sharply across her reflections. She longed to talk to him, to know all that had happened. Automatically, the memory of Nigel dancing with Anita flashed into her mind. How long had they been in touch with each other? The more she contemplated the problems, the greater and more insoluble they became. At last, after pottering aimlessly, she got into bed, trembling and tense. Every sound in the house was magnified; every creaking board making her jump. Finally, she heard Nigel come into the bathroom and, after a short while, leave it and close the door behind him. It suddenly

occurred to her that there was not a telephone in the adjoining room and that, should
the phone ring beside her bed, she would
have to disturb him. In the morning she
would make arrangements to change rooms.
In addition she wanted so to plan that Mrs
Mortimer and Mrs Pringle were not aware of
the arrangement. She, herself, always made
the bed, therefore it would be simple merely
to sleep in the dressing-room, while leaving
everything else exactly as it was at the
moment. What they might suspect was one
thing; the spoken word was an entirely different matter. Her last thought before going to
sleep was that she must unearth the Teas
Made... The problem of the laundry for the
extra sheets was simple; she always attended
to it. Concentrating on the mundane domestic issues cut across all depth of feeling; she
might have been watching a play on
television with the picture out of focus...

14

The rush of January ailments, and the start of a flu epidemic, made it impossible for Carolyn and Max to have any time alone together in which to discuss anything other than the work on hand. Surgeries were heavy; the visiting lists long. The weather was helpful for travelling, but muggy, and a breeding ground for germs. At the end of each day they almost fell into bed, exhausted.

Carolyn welcomed the pace. It enabled her to live like an automatom, reacting only to the urgency of the tasks on hand. Once or twice there had been a momentary lull, and Max had allowed his eyes to meet hers in a mute expression of love that had steadily deepened, revealing a completely new horizon. And then the moment came when, after dinner one evening, they faced each other from their respective chairs, which were drawn close to the fire. Nigel was out at a confinement, and the house became a sanctuary. Carolyn discarded a half-filled coffee cup, and looked at Max intently.

'I don't have to tell you,' he began, 'how much I've wanted to talk to you. But I couldn't risk an unfinished conversation.'

'I understood that.' It was amazing she thought, how little they had needed to put into words.

'I shall be moving into the cottage next week.' He sighed. 'I know it is the right thing, but I hate the idea more every day.'

Carolyn's expression spoke for her.

'What you must know,' he went on, 'is that I settled the problem I mentioned to you.'

She felt that some invisible power was drawing her to him, rather like an attachment from her heart to his. It made her tremble, and yet she continued to look at him unafraid of all he might see in her eyes.

'I'm glad.'

'Not,' he added, his love for her demanding such honesty as was possible, 'in my opinion, altogether honourably, Carolyn. Only marriage could really have done that. The fact that it was not acceptable does not exonerate me. I'd tell you all the details, but I'm not justified in betraying, as it were, the other person.' His voice was unsteady and she knew he was upset. 'It's difficult not to seem priggish – to myself, that is. I just don't want any unnecessary distortion.'

Carolyn glanced down at the fire. 'You didn't have to tell me any part of the truth,' she suggested gently. 'And you can hardly marry someone unwilling to marry you – no matter what the circumstances.

He made a little gesture that was self-deprecating. 'Willingness can be a matter of timing.'

'Is she all right, Max?' The question was asked earnestly.

'Yes.'

'Marriage requires a great deal of love. Conscience–'

He could not help interrupting, 'She said she did not want to marry my conscience. She wasn't bitter or accusing.' There was bewilderment in his voice.

'People can sometimes suffer more by not being allowed to make noble gestures than to make them and be absolved. Nothing works that isn't emotionally sound, in any case. Leaving the book open won't help either of you. She must be very wise.'

'So are you, and very tolerant.'

Carolyn sighed. 'No, Max – vulnerable.' It was not what she meant to say, but the word was the only truth she knew at that moment.

The silence was filled with unspoken words. A log fell off the fire on to the hearth. Max slipped down on one knee, picked up the tongs, and replaced it so that sparks leaped up the chimney and new flames spurted to increase the blaze.

Carolyn knew that she did not want him to return to his chair; she wanted his arms around her. If he had reached out, even to touch her hand, will power would have vanished.

'How much does that word "vulnerable" tell me?' he asked as he sat back again.

'As much as it possibly can in the circumstances.' Her voice trembled.

He looked at her and he knew he could not just leave things as they were. 'You do not sleep with Nigel, do you?'

'No.' She was relieved by the quiet directness of the question.

'Oh, *Carolyn!*' He spoke with a savage frustration.

'Perhaps,' she said revealingly, 'I ask too much, and am too emotional.'

His voice was low and tender. 'You are a very wonderful person.'

His words were like music to her, music drifting into the dead, silent world in which she seemed to have lived so long. The shadows in the room vanished, and all the fire and passion of loving, and being loved, enveloped them inescapably.

Neither was conscious of moving. His arms reached out and she gave herself up to the ecstasy, lost to everything beyond the overwhelming need of a desire shared.

'What,' he asked, as they sat down again, 'are we going to do?' Already the sharp agony of hurt pierced his heart as he thought of Nigel. Nothing could alter the fact that he was her husband.

'Just for a little while, not even to think,' she answered simply.

'I love you far more than I ever believed myself capable of loving.'

How often, Carolyn thought, had she ached to hear Nigel utter similar words? *I must learn how to make pretty speeches.* His remark came back – the echo from New Year's Eve.

Max spoke hastily. 'You don't have to tell me anything. There is so much I know, and so much I am afraid to hear.'

'As I suppose I am afraid to repeat words I've uttered before. All I know is that, as we sit here like this, I feel I am living in a new dimension, where everything glows and I am alive again.' Her voice was shaky. 'I wanted you to love me. I wanted your arms around me.' Faint colour tinged her cheeks, and her heart beats were uneven as she cried, 'I shall miss you so *much.*'

'I shall be here every day and perhaps, sometimes, we can meet.' There was an unconscious pleading in the suggestion.

Carolyn resisted the impulse to ask about the past and Anita.

'I'd love to have dinner with you,' she said quietly. 'I'd love to go to The White Hart in Lewes, with its candlelight and flowers. Its atmosphere.'

'Then, no matter what happens, we must go there together.' Max remembered Moreen in that second with a great humility. He added, almost abruptly, 'Always trust me, Carolyn.'

'I will,' she promised with conviction. As she spoke, a strange sensation crept over her. She was talking as though their future was inextricably interwoven. The words they had uttered could not be retracted; they could not return to their former evasions where emotion lay explosively just beneath the surface of conversation. The thought of Nigel brought apathy. She was in no mood to analyse, or to justify, the excitement of her present happiness.

Neither of them spoiled the perfection of the moments left to them before Nigel returned. They remained in their respective chairs, exchanging anecdotes, laughing, and suddenly lapsing into silence…

Nigel's car drove into the garage and he appeared in the room soon afterwards, stopping on the threshold and, without being aware of doing so, looking from face to face. It seemed to him that the air was charged with electricity and its current was tingling though him. In that moment, his last doubt vanished. They were in love with each other.

'Something wrong with the damned car,' he said shortly. 'Exhaust, I think. Rumbles like an empty stomach.' He went to the cocktail cabinet and poured himself a generous brandy. 'Nothing to eat, thanks.' He turned, and answered Carolyn's question before she had asked it. 'Any calls?'

'Perfect silence,' said Max.

Nigel was trying not to think, but the picture of them sitting there – the fire glowing and spluttering as Carolyn threw on two more logs – made him a stranger in his own house, Sun, and the warmth of a summer evening, could not have emphasised the fact half so much as this intimate winter scene. He flopped down on the sofa, ignoring his own particular chair. Not to make the gesture obvious, he lifted one leg and stretched it full length on the cushions.

'Tired?' Carolyn asked.

'But – *always,*' he replied meaningly.

She flushed slightly, and his eyes met hers. His imperceptible smile was a trifle ironic. Her remark held all the sympathy of guilt.

'Easy case?' Max lit a cigarette.

'Very. Ideal couple to have children.' He looked at Carolyn. 'By the way, I presume you know that Freda returns home tomorrow.'

'Far longer job than was originally expected,' Max put in quickly.

'But you did say she was all right,' Carolyn exclaimed. 'I rang her today, as usual, and she said she was fine.'

'I kept her in for a much needed rest. For once, she had to do as she was told.' And all the time he was speaking, Nigel was assessing the situation between Max and Carolyn, his nerves raw. Having drained his glass, he got to his feet. 'I've a report to work on.' With that he went into his consulting room, sat down at his desk, and held his head in his hands. Where, he asked himself, did he go from here?

The telephone rang and he answered it, grateful for the distraction.

'Anita… Yes, quite alone.' He glanced at his watch. It was nine-thirty. 'I'll be with you in half an hour…' He was very calm as, a matter of minutes later, he opened the sitting-room door and said, 'I'm going out. Probably be late. Good night.' He glanced across at Max. 'Will you take any calls?'

'Of course.'

Carolyn made no comment. But she thought of Anita.

Anita said, 'I was right, Nigel, wasn't I?'

He nodded, and dug himself more deeply into his chair. He could not have said just why he was there. 'I'm sorry I misjudged you.'

'That's all right. These things happen.'

Nigel felt suddenly homeless. He took the drink she handed him and let his gaze wander about the room. Everything had a permanency which Downs Cottage had lost. 'What did you want to see me about?'

'Nothing really,' she admitted. 'I was going to make my party the excuse.'

'Party?' The word sounded absurd.

'You remember New Year's Eve when it was arranged. I spoke to Freda today.'

'I remember New Year's Eve,' he echoed grimly.

Now that he was with her, Anita wanted to help. The strange quirk of emotion putting her own desires aside in the protective endeavour to comfort him. 'Are you quite sure?' Her eyes met his anxiously. 'I mean just because I was beastly enough to implant doubt in your mind...'

'You succeeded in that.' There was no compromise in his voice. 'This is different. I should have thought you'd be delighted.'

'I'm not. I don't understand myself, so I cannot expect you to understand me. All I know is that your pain is mine. I'd hate triumph on those terms.'

He stared at her bewildered, shaking his head. 'I had to talk to someone. The trouble with life is that having taken one foolhardy step, one leaps to another.'

Anita winced. 'Referring to me?'

'No.' It was strange, he thought, that in the chaos of the present, he could seek understanding from the past. 'You told me that Carolyn was starved of emotion. How could you possibly know?'

'Call it a silent language spoken by women, if you like. You have only to look at Carolyn to realise that she is a vibrant, passionate type.'

Her words grated. 'Was that why you suggested Max was far more her type than I?'

'Not altogether. If I recall rightly, I said that she was just as starved of emotion as you. But you have a forbidding air about you these days. A chip on your shoulder if you like.'

'That's utter nonsense.'

She got up, walked behind his chair and, leaning over, touched his forehead with her lips. 'But you'll have to come to terms with yourself before you can solve any problems.'

'I wish to heaven I could see straight.'

She moved restlessly away to the window and, parting the curtains, looked down the square to the sea. There was tumult within her, and a sickness, too.

'You can't,' she said briefly, 'because you feel about Carolyn as I feel about you.' She turned away from the window and sank down in her chair. 'I came here because I believed that I could get you back in my own way. I'm either a bigger fool than I took myself to be, or slightly better than I'd be given credit for.' Her eyes met his with disarming frankness. 'Now that Carolyn no longer loves you, I can bear the situation.'

'That hardly makes sense.'

'Not to a man; to a woman, yes.'

'Why?' He looked perplexed.

She sighed. 'A woman dislikes intensely

any other woman loving the man she, herself, loves.' Her tone changed to a breathless inquiry, 'Would you divorce her?'

'Should I be in any position to refuse? Speaking from a point of justice.' Unreality came back like a ghost haunting him. He couldn't be sitting there, in Anita's flat, confiding in her; the fact was preposterous. So was the possibility of divorce. He and Carolyn. 'How on earth can one move so far away from someone one loves? It doesn't make sense.'

'And takes two. It need not be the fault of either of them; there's nothing normal in the way people in love behave. They're not even intelligent about it.' She made a gesture and sighed. 'Look at me.'

He had not expected an attitude like this. 'Meaning that your coming here, to Hove, was crazy?'

'Yes. I became very hard, Nigel. Determined to get what I wanted. Not very bright of me when, the moment you come in here, unhappy, I behave like Goody-two-shoes. Although I'm not so far gone that I overlook the fact that if Carolyn were out of your life I might stand a chance. I'm still calculating enough for that.' She dropped her voice to a whisper, 'It's all such hell, isn't it?'

Her thoughts went back to the evening when she had sat at her dressing table, awaiting Nigel's first visit to the flat. Her determination; her assessment of her own physical assets.

'I suppose we none of us realise our capacity for jealousy until it is aroused.'

'We none of us realise anything about ourselves until we are put to some test or other.' Her eyes flashed with sudden annoyance. 'Carolyn's taken away all my weapons. Ironical, isn't it? The last thing I ever expected was that there would be someone in *her* life. I was prepared to fight her for you. Emotion is pretty primitive... I hope Max proves to be a faithful lover.'

'Lover.' Nigel was instantly defensive. 'I was not suggesting anything to do with infidelity.'

Anita smiled wryly. 'Don't delude yourself. Love hasn't any demarcation line.' As she spoke she could not reject the possibility that she and Max might find it possible to come to terms, and help each other, seeing that their aims were identical. He wanted Carolyn: she wanted Nigel.

'It can have loyalty,' Nigel snapped.

'Words can be as great a disloyalty as any physical act.'

Nigel hated the stinging truth of the statement.

'And Max has never professed to be a saint where women are concerned,' Anita insisted. 'Just the type to fall madly in love at the finish, and to be faithful... What are you going to do?'

'Nothing hastily.'

Anita curbed the sudden antagonism which took the place of understanding. The situation might harden against her. Nigel was not likely to condone Carolyn's love affair, or to give her up without a struggle.

'You are quite certain of your facts?'

'There are no facts,' he said emphatically. 'Nothing except an unshakable conviction. There are some things one *knows*.' He looked at her intently. 'Since you were so convinced of the attraction...'

She cut in quickly, 'You hold that against me?'

'When it comes to it, I suppose I do. I might have been spared the suspicion; I might have continued to deceive myself. Ignorance may be a folly, but it is comforting all the same.'

'I'm sorry.' She was genuine, particularly as he was now too wretched, and involved with his own emotions, even to notice her, other than as someone with whom he could relieve his pent-up feelings.

'Then why not go back to folly?' She spoke icily.

He glanced at his watch. 'I'd no earthly right to bother you with all this.' He was impatient with himself.

She tossed him the words, 'My shoulder is there to cry on. The situation appeals to my sense of humour.' Her eyes met his with hostility. Then, she apologised, 'Afraid Goody-two-shoes can't stay the course. At this moment I hate you for loving her. I know; without any right whatsoever.'

'Rights, hate, love.' His cracked laughter died into silence. 'Thank you for putting up with me.'

Her mood changed, softened by his words and expression. 'Please come again.'

Reaching the square a few moments later, he felt an isolation which made the night darker, and the sea more cruel.

15

The silence that came to Downs Cottage lay behind every sound and every activity within it. Mrs Mortimer and Mrs Pringle exchanged glances over a pile of groceries that had just been delivered. 'Nothing's the same,' said Mrs Pringle. Her expression was serious. 'Doctor never used to be bad tempered, but he is now. He doesn't look well, either.'

'No; he doesn't look well.' Mrs Mortimer sighed. 'February isn't a good month. I hate February, but let's hope it will be better than January.'

'At least the epidemic has died down.' They were avoiding the subject uppermost in their minds.

At last Mrs Pringle said, 'Seems strange without Doctor Faber.'

'I expect he's glad to have a place of his own. Most people are... When you've finished the dining-room we'd better start on Doctor Faber's room, and get it ready for Doctor Blake.'

Mrs Pringle nodded. There was the sadness of understanding in her eyes. Both she and Mrs Mortimer had known about the sleeping arrangements almost from the moment they had been altered. This was different. They could neither deceive themselves, nor each other, now that the doctor was moving to the other side of the house.

They later transferred all the personal items and hung Nigel's suits in the large compactum, neatly placing his shirts in their special trays, and his many ties on the rack fitment.

'Makes the house seem like an institution,' Mrs Pringle murmured, half to herself.

Mrs Mortimer paused at the large windows and looked out over the downs to Firlie Beacon where the sun filtered through a winter haze. A dog barked on an adjoining farm; cattle grazed in a distant field. But there was not a complete picture – just a series of observations, as though even the country had detached itself, and was part of a foreign scene.

The sound of the typewriter broke the silence rather like muted machine gun fire.

Their task finished, the two women stood and looked about them. They did not comment further because their feelings were sufficiently sincere to rise above gossip.

'I can hear the doctor's car,' said Mrs Mortimer. 'I'd better go and make the coffee.'

Nigel came in from his rounds and opened the door of Carolyn's room. 'If you could do a few letters.'

Carolyn picked up her note pad.

'We'll go next door,' he said hurriedly, not wanting to sit in the chair that Max invariably occupied when he needed any work done.

Mrs Mortimer brought in the coffee. Carolyn refused hers; Nigel was grateful for his.

'By the way,' Carolyn said quickly, 'you'll find everything in order where your room is concerned.'

'Thank you. I'm sure I shall.' He was poker faced.

The letters were routine, and when he had finished dictating he asked, 'When is Max coming in again? I must discuss the Harrington case with him. Difficult family that – trouble makers. If they had their way we'd both be on call twenty-four hours a day. He has taken them over because he is nearer than I. Jim Harrington has a foul, insulting temper; no time for his wife, but wants to keep her alive because she's a good cook-housekeeper. Her death would inconvenience him.'

'A diabetic, isn't she?'

'Yes.' Nigel drank the last of his coffee. 'Max may be able to cope with them better than I.' He shot at her, 'It probably seems strange to you without him in the house!'

'It does... I invited Anita for a meal tomorrow night.'

He stared at her with astonishment and suspicion. 'Why?'

'She rang up about her invitation to the party she mentioned at New Year. Also, she is going to be over here seeing friends.' Carolyn's manner was off-hand. 'I thought you would approve the idea.'

'I might, if I felt you liked her.' Their eyes met warily.

'I prefer dinner here, to the party effort... That does not prevent your accepting.'

'I see.' Jealousy flamed. 'There are some irritations you will have to bear. Accompanying me to various functions is one of them.'

'Very well.' Her voice was subdued.

'Freda and David will be there. Anita said—' He stopped abruptly.

Carolyn got up from her chair. He might not have spoken. 'I'll get these done,' she said, flicking over the pages, 'so that you can sign them before you go to hospital.'

Was this her way of putting him in the wrong because of all she felt for Max? Inviting *Anita* to dinner. His thoughts stopped racing in what he realised might be the wrong direction. Probably Anita slid the idea into her mind and gave her no alternative. Nigel faced the fact that he had not the courage to ask her about Max. Once the matter was discussed he would have to force an issue. A blind had been pulled down in their marriage, and he was stumbling about with sightless eyes. Yet she was strangely calm, almost detached, and without any visible signs of suffering. She asked only questions concerning his physical well being, and when he had requested that Max's vacated room should be made ready for him because it would be simpler for them both, she had made no comment other than to tell him she would give Mrs Mortimer the instructions. It no longer mattered about the change in their relationship being obvious. All the same, it had offered him an excellent opportunity to challenge her; to make her realise what their separation meant to him, emotionally, physically, mentally. Yet he had not made love to her for some time before their final parting. He tried to understand why. Not lack of desire; but the weight of guilt and uncertainty involving Max and Anita. And added to this, her own aloofness because of his secrecy over Max's appointment. Looking back, remembering his taunts, and hers, was like drawing a rasp over torn flesh. Disintegration of a marriage. He had watched so many, and knew that so few had been wrecked by dramatic issues, or great tragedy; but by a slow process of petty misunderstandings. Even now, aware of her feelings for Max, he could not face up to the final shattering blow of losing her. Equally, he had no words with which to lure her back.

He had become a man petrified by the smouldering desire of his love for her. Everything he had taken for granted was in jeopardy. Proximity was a torment which explained why he was moving into a room as far away as possible from her.

There was a passionate hunger in his eyes as he watched her. She had turned at the door. 'I didn't ask if you'll be in for lunch?'

'Yes; there are several things – apart from the Harringtons – I want to discuss with Max.'

Carolyn's heart was beating unevenly. What things? 'Oh,' she exclaimed, 'the telephones are in order so that we have the extension working. Fortunately we are in the same exchange area, or it would not have been possible.' She added, 'I had the switch gadget put in my room.'

'Why your room?' So that she could be in constant touch with Max?

'Because I can take any messages when Max switches over to us before he goes out.' Her voice was without emotion. 'Also to prevent your being disturbed in the middle of a consultation. I have the ordinary switch board in my room, too, and for the same reason.'

He felt mean. 'Don't know how you cope with any of them.'

'Simple once you grasp it.'

She returned to her desk. Sub-consciously

she was listening for the sound of Max's voice. Typing had become automatic and her speed was now almost that of an expert. The extension between Downs Cottage and Max's rang, the buzzer startling and unfamiliar to her. He said, his voice exciting her, 'Would you tell Nigel I'll be in about two?'

'Yes... You have three appointments here during the afternoon.'

'Thank heaven for patients!'

'I agree.' There was so much she wanted to say but emotion silenced her.

'I'm switching the phone over to you after this call... What are you doing? Stupid question.'

'Typing.' She gave a little laugh, 'and doodling.' Replacing the receiver, she glanced up and saw Nigel standing in the doorway.

'Max will be in about two.'

'There's a letter for him.' Nigel handed her the envelope. 'Better keep it so that it does not get mixed up with ours.'

Carolyn took it and put it aside. It struck her that it was addressed in Max's own handwriting. 'I've finished all this.' She pulled the last sheets of paper from the typewriter. Nigel still stood there watching, hating to move away. He noticed her dress, which was his favourite shade of blue. Her hair shone and her skin glowed and, as she looked at him, some part of their past seemed to flash between them. A little un-nerved, she collected all the correspondence and preceded him into his consulting room.

'I never realised just how efficient a secretary you really were,' he said, as he began to sign the letters which she placed on his large blotting pad.

'There were many things about me you didn't realise.'

It was the first personal observation she had made for a long while. He glanced up from his task. 'I agree. It could also be true in reverse.' The words 'You love him, don't you?' were on his tongue, but he could not bring himself to utter them. He waited for her comment which, when it came, shocked him.

'Perhaps I realised too well, Nigel.' There was an unfamiliarity about her use of his name. They had managed to avoid any mode of address since endearments vanished from their relationship. 'That will be Mrs Pearson. Blood test. You want to take the sample to hospital.'

He nodded, the moment of conversation over. 'I'd be grateful if you would remain with her. She's an hysteric.'

Carolyn donned her white coat and went out to greet the patient, surprised to find that she was not more than about thirty. Elegant, petulant, and spoiled.

'I can't stand pain,' she began, staring at

Carolyn and faintly jealous of her attractiveness. That was her prerogative; no one else
must, even remotely, provide competition. 'I
haven't seen you before?' she asked. 'New?'

'Not really; I'm Dr Blake's wife.'

'Oh.' The thin lips went down a little more
at the corner.

Another one, thought Carolyn, who
wanted to see herself as a pet patient for
whom the doctor had a secret desire. A wife
could be a hindrance, especially when in
attendance! For all that, Mrs Pearson cooed
the moment she saw Nigel, adopting an
accent of pseudo Mayfair, but dropping
back to a natural suburban variety only
when about – as she thought – to be hurt.

'A needle in a vein,' she exclaimed. 'Must
I?' She raised her heavily made-up eyes to
Nigel's. 'I can't stand the sight of blood.'

'Then don't look. It is only a matter of
drawing a little off.' He tried to curb his
impatience.

'I shall be able to go to a party tonight?'

Nigel would have loved to say, 'You'll live,'
but merely nodded.

'The Wilders and my husband and I are
going to Eastbourne – to the Grand... Do
you know the Wilders? But of course you do.'

Carolyn applied the surgical spirit and
discarded the swab of cotton wool. Mrs
Wilder. How well she recalled that night...
The night when Nigel came home and said,

'I can't go on like this.'

It was not necessary for Nigel to comment about Mrs Wilder because he was informed that Doctor Faber now took care of her, and what a very nice doctor he was, and how she understood he had moved near Beddingham.

'Now,' said Carolyn, 'if you will keep the arm quite still.'

Fortunately the vein obliged by taking the needle as thought it belonged there, much to Mrs Pearson's relief, and disappointment. A little drama would not have been amiss. She left, cooing again, lifting the collar of her mink coat a little nearer her face as she went out to the Rolls that awaited her.

'Another major operation over.' Carolyn tidied up. 'The doctor's wife is not always popular with the patients.'

Nigel said quietly, 'So long as she is popular with the doctor.'

Carolyn stared at him for a second. There was nothing responsive in her attitude, and she made him feel that his remark had been ridiculous. She handed him a large envelope. 'The X-rays of Mark Gorton. You asked me to remind you.'

He took them. 'Wellings will want a lung resection. I'm worried about the case.'

Carolyn removed her white coat. She was conscious of Nigel's gaze upon her and a little unnerved by it. He left the house and she was grateful. There was no question in her mind about the near future; the situation between them could not continue as it was. In theory, nothing could be simpler than the break up of marriage when both parties were involved elsewhere. In practice, it was a very different matter, particularly as so much in Nigel's life was a mystery to her.

When Max arrived, Carolyn had already eaten alone. Nigel could not get back.

'Beastly business, eating alone,' Max said, half in disgust. 'Beastly business being alone, too.'

They looked at each other in silent understanding. Max put out a hand and clasped hers. 'There is so much I want to discuss with you. It's hopeless here.'

She read his thoughts. 'I'll come over to you the moment we can arrange things.'

Max lit a cigarette; his hands were trembling.

'I must tell him, Carolyn.'

'I know... Do you think he is in love with Anita?'

'Anita.' Max was startled.

'I haven't pried, and I'm only asking for your opinion.' Her gaze was steady and inescapable.

'I haven't any opinion. I just hope he is.'

'A woman's intuition can only go so far... He sees her.'

'Do you mind?' Jealousy underlined the question.

'It would be hypocritical if I did. I suppose nothing is quite real any more.'

'Was your marriage real before–' He paused for a second and then added – 'us?'

'You know it wasn't.'

'Have you missed my living here these few days?'

'Dreadfully.'

'I was afraid you might not.' His gaze travelled over her face.

'Nigel is moving into your room.' The words brought momentary silence between them.

'Mrs Pringle and Mrs Mortimer–' He stopped.

'Mrs Mortimer looked sad. That was all. It hurt me.'

They tried to prevent tension building up; to ignore emotion. Carolyn said abruptly, 'There's a letter for you. On my desk over there.'

Max picked it up and after a hasty glance, thrust it into his pocket. The sudden strain on his face did not escape her.

Nigel returned from the hospital and asked for sandwiches and coffee. He began talking to Max, finally coming to the Harringtons. 'I want to warn you about them. Put one wrong foot forward, and they'll haul you up before the Executive Council.'

'Like that, is it?'

'Exactly.'

'Is that why you've turned them over to me?'

'Perhaps.' Nigel stared him out. 'I couldn't stand Harrington's temper, and since you are that much nearer...'

Max crossed one leg over the other. 'I found him quite reasonable. Anxious about his wife.'

'Splendid.' Nigel ate the last sandwich. 'Long may the honeymoon last.' It was his way of dismissing the subject. He went on, 'I had sad news of Moreen Fuller this morning.'

Max moistened his lips with his tongue; his mouth suddenly dry.

Carolyn cried, her voice breathless, 'You don't mean–'

'She fell down the stone steps leading from her aunt's flat. They rushed her to hospital, but she lost the child.'

Max could not speak. The child was *his*.

Nigel lit a cigarette. 'One never knows in these cases whether it is a good thing or a bad. The prospective adoptive parents will be shattered.'

'And – and Moreen Fuller?'

'Shock and a broken arm.' Nigel saw an expression in Max's eyes which reminded him of the episode when Moreen fainted. Was there some link between the two of them? Or was that the suspicion of sheer prejudice on his part?

'I'm so sorry,' Carolyn said, 'and thankful she is all right. It has always seemed a specially sad case.'

Max's hand had gone instinctively into his pocket. He was not prepared for the overwhelming guilt that lay upon him. His memories were unbearably poignant, and he knew he could not sit there and utter empty comments. He got up from his chair. 'Work,' he said jerkily, and went from the room.

Carolyn felt that an icy hand had touched her heart. A sickness went over her. She knew, then, that the girl in Max's past was Moreen Fuller...

'He's not very sympathetic,' Nigel exclaimed deliberately.

'You'll be going to see her?'

'Yes.'

'I'd like to send her some flowers. You obviously know the hospital.'

'All the particulars are in her file. And the address of her aunt, Mrs Cole.'

'When did this happen?'

'Three days ago. I had the news from her father when I called in this morning. He was coming to see me this evening, after going up to see Moreen. Mrs Cole didn't tell him immediately it happened – rightly or wrongly – she wanted to spare him until they knew everything was all right.'

Carolyn was hearing without listening, the words a background for her thoughts.

The afternoon brought its work which Carolyn did automatically, putting the case notes back as the patients left, attending to all the instruments, setting up the sterile trolley and managing to get in some correspondence which she could answer herself. She needed only to show Max's patients into his consulting room, their complaints uncomplicated, and follow ups from previous examinations. It was not until about half an hour before surgery began that they had a brief while to themselves. Nigel was out, and Mrs Mortimer brought in the tea saying, 'I thought you might like this.' She had made small sandwiches, which neither Carolyn nor Max felt like eating, and yet dare not leave because it would seem unappreciative. Suddenly, almost abruptly, Max said jerkily, 'You know, don't you?' His face had a tinge of grey, and his eyes a hunted look.

Carolyn was trembling. 'Yes; I can't tell you how. I'd no idea before. Just something in your attitude.'

He looked at her with unconscious appeal. 'How much difference does it make, Carolyn?'

'I don't think any. Shock, yes. If you had not told me anything about the situation I should have despised you.'

'I despise myself. It's terrifying how cowardly one can be.'

Their eyes met in silent questioning before she said, 'Do you think she might marry you now?'

He was startled. 'Meaning you believe I ought to marry her?'

Carolyn felt miserably uncertain.

Max spoke firmly. 'It wouldn't work. It wouldn't right the initial wrong, and now that the – the child is not there to provide a reason, we'd be two people bound together by dark memories.' He took the letter from his pocket.

Carolyn read, 'Am writing this with my left hand so hope you can read it. Don't worry. I'm all right, and nothing has changed for us because I've lost the baby. I shall never forget you; but I know there is happiness for me somewhere. Remember me sometimes. Moreen.'

A tear dropped from Carolyn's cheek on to the sheet of paper. She didn't speak. All the words had been said.

16

Carolyn did not make any secret of the fact that she was going over to visit Max, and to see his cottage for the first time. 'It sounds a very interesting old place,' she said with enthusiasm.

Nigel remarked stiffly, 'I am sure you will find it so.' He did not ask when, or at what time, she proposed to go, thus avoiding the pain of suspense.

It was a mild, late February evening when Carolyn set off from Downs Cottage just as the sun was setting. Winter might, capriciously, have allowed a breath of spring to touch the countryside, which lay serene beneath the reflected glory of a crimson sky; the downs rising impressively against the rifting, rainbow-tipped clouds. As she drove the very short distance, the peace of the landscape touched her with the magic of quietude. For those few moments she belonged only to herself.

She saw Max standing beside a lych-type gate the moment she turned into the lane to which he had directed her. For, while he was so near the Lewes-Polgate Road, he was hidden from prying eyes, and although that might have been a great disadvantage from the point of view of his patients, they were safeguarded by the fact that everyone in the district knew Knoll Cottage, because its owner was very wealthy and very eccentric. The seclusion, therefore, was of a geographical nature.

Dusk shimmered into gentle blue darkness as the car stopped. The silence was deep as their hands touched while they walked together down the flagged pathway to the open front door which led into a large sitting room, softly lit by golden-shaded lamps. There was a smell of old books and parchments, and of furniture that was steeped in the atmosphere of the past; the grandfather clock ticked into a silence that lingered from yesterday.

Max slid Carolyn's coat from her shoulders and threw it across a nearby chair. 'I love you – desperately.' His gaze lowered from her eyes to her lips, and his arms closed around her. 'I've dreamed of this for so long,' he whispered.

Carolyn did not draw back. When at last his mouth lifted from hers, she was helpless against the emotion surging through her. They sat down on the sofa together, his hand clasping hers, returning to the point where he had asked, 'What are we going to do?' Only now, they both knew they could not continue without reaching a final decision. Work, circumstances, had enabled time to be on lease to them. Max looked grave. 'I must not do the wrong thing.'

She shrank back a little and he hastened, 'I'm thinking of you. I do not need to think of myself. No matter what it might involve, nothing could change my feelings, or my desires.'

Carolyn was trembling as she said, 'An empty marriage is mockery. Emptier than being alone. But you're both doctors. It isn't like dealing with business people.'

'You are not my patient,' Max reminded her.

'I shouldn't help your career by involving you in a divorce case.'

His fingers tightened round her hand.

'Suppose you allow me to worry about that.'

'And there's your work... I mean yours and Nigel's.' The distress in her eyes made them seem darker and larger.

Max gave a little hollow laugh. 'My darling, I could not go on with Nigel in any case – whatever our decision. Any more than he would want me to. The idea is fantastic.'

'I know that. What I don't know, or cannot see, is how best to plan with the least hurt to everyone.'

'"Everyone" being Nigel?' The question came abruptly.

'No.' Her eyes were wide and helpless.

'I'm sure he wants to be free as much as I do.'

'Would it make any difference if it were otherwise?' Max was looking at her intently.

Honesty forced her to say, 'Yes; it would impose responsibility, no matter what had happened between us.'

Reluctantly Max agreed.

'It isn't what one does, so much as how one does it,' she insisted. 'I just want to be sure that he is involved with Anita. Oh, not so that I could whitewash myself because of my feelings, but because, then, we could both help each other and behave like rational civilised people.'

Max listened carefully, the past parading like a mocking ghost. 'In that case it is simple enough to ask him for the truth.'

'You see,' she said, ruefully, shaking her head, 'where scruple leads you. Could I ask him for the truth without being honest myself?'

'Well?' Max insisted. 'Could you?'

'No.' Her voice was resolute.

Max picked up her hand and kissed it. 'Then that's settled.'

Her gaze wandered anxiously over his face. 'You agree?'

'Whole-heartedly.' He paused significantly. 'Except that I don't want you to have to stand up to this alone. I'm more than ready to tell him at any time.'

Carolyn shook her head. 'I shall make your feelings quite clear.'

'I doubt if you could ever do that.' His voice was low and seemed to throb into silence. 'Until now I have made light of love; perhaps this is my lesson.'

'We all learn the hard way, really.' She looked into the fire (lit specially for her), and a flash-back from childhood created faces in the white hot coal, and the pin points of sparks clinging to the soot at the back of the grate were the soldiers she had loved to watch as she sat on her mother's knee in the twilight. Now, here she was discussing the break up of her marriage.

Max leaned towards her, anxiety and apprehension in his manner. 'Would you be prepared to leave England – live abroad?'

She answered without hesitation, 'Yes, it would be the best way.'

He shook his head almost in bewilderment. 'I can't believe that, knowing all you do about me, you are willing to give up everything even to leaving England.'

Her gaze was very direct. 'I really do know all about you, don't I, Max?'

'Everything to my detriment,' he answered truthfully.

'I could not bear to live with any more shadows; any more secrets. They are like rust eating away everything worth while. I'm afraid I've no confessions to make.' She gave a little laugh that held a touch of self-deprecation. 'Oh, I had the usual ecstatically happy, and desperately unhappy, crushes, but that's all. Perhaps that is what made me rather stupid when it came to marriage.'

'Stupid?' The echo was indignant.

'I wanted at least *some* of the honeymoon to continue. And that makes me sound very corny and immature. I shall never be just a cook-housekeeper, Max – never. I'll go anywhere, do everything I can to help you. I'll willingly take over the domestic chores, and cooking, just so long as you do not ignore me as a woman. Doctor, or no doctor. And I don't mean the ridiculous nonsense about forgetting anniversaries, or birthdays. I mean being mentally close as well as physically.' She added, 'I believe I'm a perfectly normal woman sexually, and if you are the type later on to look at me without ever seeing me, then things will never work between us, either.' She was roused almost to the point of anger as memories crowded back. 'Oh, I know that now emotion is uppermost. I don't want it to die after marriage, that's all.' She paused, fearful lest her outburst had been unjust. 'It would not be fair to say things were always as I have indirectly painted them.'

'Only since my advent?' There was a trace of nervousness in the question.

'Before then. And if a man hasn't faith

enough in his wife to confide in her, how can he expect marriage to work?' she added bitterly. 'The past is one thing; but when it spills over into the present and clouds the future, then it becomes impossible. I know there is something between Nigel and Anita – something from the past. That makes their present relationship all the more important and impossible to accept.' She held Max's gaze. 'And my intuition tells me that you know all about this.'

'My knowledge ends with the past.'

They looked into each other's eyes and silence fell between them. He drew her into his arms so that her head rested against his shoulder. Then he lowered his lips to hers.

'And now,' he said a little later, 'I am going to take you to dinner at The White Hart.'

'Tonight?' There was excitement in her voice.

'Yes. If we are seen by any of the grape vine enthusiasts, it won't matter because Nigel will soon be in the picture.'

Carolyn nodded her agreement. Everything was strange and unreal, as though she had wandered into a new world. When she went upstairs to the bathroom before leaving the cottage, she felt that only her body was moving about, while her mind was a blank. Everything was a matter of impression; a stimulation of the senses. The smell of 'after shave' lotion hung in the atmosphere, noticeable to her since Nigel's things had gone from what had once been *their* bathroom. Here, there was no woman's touch, no compromise. Gleaming white tiles, and a very large bath, suggested to her the austerity of a hospital. Possibly, she thought, without knowing quite why, there was always an odd, self-conscious feeling about using a bathroom not one's own, as though every act could be witnessed by those in the rest of the house.

'Is this the type of house you like to live in?' She asked the question as she joined Max in the sitting-room.

'The type I would like to have *as well as*.'

'Meaning London and a country cottage.'

'I suppose that is as near the truth as I can get. Never having lived in the country for long, perhaps I'm afraid of it all the year round.' His smile transformed his face. 'But I'd live anywhere so long as you were with me – and you were happy.'

They went out to the car and looked up at the night sky where a crescent moon lay against the gentle darkness like a jewel glittering on velvet. There was no wind and the trees stood majestic and a little eerie. Frost had formed on the grass verge outside the cottage gate; it made a crackling sound as they walked the few paces. Max looked around him. 'I shall never forget this cottage – never, my darling,' he said softly as he saw

Carolyn into the car and closed the door. A moment later headlights threw a beam of light into the darkness; a rabbit scuttled and disappeared. Furrows in the lane ahead led the way to a nearby farm, its lighted windows like friendly eyes looking out from the snugness of home.

It was a very short drive into Lewes, and The White Hart Hotel on the south side of the High Street gleamed white in the darkness.

'I've been here before,' Carolyn said, 'but it was a long time ago.'

'It boasts an excellent night porter,' Max said, 'named Charles, who doesn't hover round if you stay up talking half the night, or give you a sour look if you want drinks and sandwiches. I stayed here about six months ago – just for a night... Let's have a drink in the cocktail lounge.' He added, 'I've already booked a table.'

Carolyn glanced around her, the mustardy-gold carpet was bright without being garish, and she relaxed, shutting out conflict and looking into Max's eyes as she raised her dry Martini.

'To many years of these,' he murmured. 'Hungry?'

'Very.' She realised that she had hardly eaten a proper meal for days, and that food had seemed like chaff in her mouth which was perpetually dry.

'I've already ordered duck with orange sauce. It will be ready when we are. And smoked salmon to begin with.' His smile was broad. 'Not very clever of me, because I happen to know you like both.'

'Um-m.' She brightened. 'A meal one does not have to choose is always fun. I look down the vast menus and never know what I really want until the person at the next table has something I've overlooked, and wish I'd chosen!'

They went into the large dining-room. Sconces holding two red candles – a flower arrangement round them – decorated each table so that the glow cast soft shadows upon the pine panelling. Heavy curtains fell from the long windows to a green carpet, which was streaked with black.

'This has an air of a London restaurant, without any of the noise or tables set so close together that one can reach the other person's side plate just as easily as one's own!' Carolyn exclaimed. 'To say nothing of having smoke blown perpetually in one's face... I don't know why we haven't been here more often.' She stopped. It was so obvious that the plural meant Nigel.

'I'm very glad of the omission.'

The smoked salmon was perfect, as was the Aylesbury duckling. Carolyn ate every mouthful. The wine Max chose was a 1959 Chambertin, and they toasted each other in silence with a look sharpened by desire. There were no clocks in their world and no tomorrow; only the precious moment holding the enchantment of a stolen hour. The candles flickered over Carolyn's face, putting stars in her eyes and emphasising the beauty of her face and bone structure.

'No piped music; no strident band,' she said reflectively. 'It is so difficult to find somewhere peaceful, with all the excitement of a romantic setting without perpetual noise. I hate competing against deafening sound. Must be getting old.' Her laughter held a note of sadness. The little trap door of memory burst open at that moment, and her heart was stabbed by the realisation of Nigel's indifference, and of all the upheaval about to be faced.

'Will you always remember coming here?' His voice was low.

'Always. It is when one forgets and everything is doomed by sameness...'

Max glanced suddenly at his watch. 'I must take you back.' He tried to keep emotion from his voice by speaking quickly, almost abruptly. 'We've been here nearly three hours.' Before asking for his bill, he said urgently, 'Carolyn, you're everything I looked for. Exciting and yet restful, and your understanding... What *should* I have done without it? I shall bless you for that always.'

They drove back to Knoll Cottage.

Carolyn refused to allow Max to return with her.

'I can follow you there – *be* there,' he insisted.

'I'd rather not. I shall probably wait until tomorrow before I discuss things.'

Max was looking at her with a deep longing as she added, 'It is like waiting for a thunder storm to break.'

They looked back at the cottage which was now a dim shape in the darkness. Carolyn got into her car. Max stood at the open door and leaned forward to kiss her lips. 'Go quickly,' he said.

17

Nigel arrived home that evening to find a flustered Mrs Mortimer running out to the garage to meet him.

'I've only just come in, Doctor. It was arranged that I might have the evening off, seeing that you and Mrs Blake were going to be out–' She paused for breath. 'There was a man hammering on the door when I got back. Very abusive. He's waiting for you now in the sitting-room. Wouldn't give his name.'

'Thank you, Mrs Mortimer. I'll attend to him.' It was obvious that Carolyn had not yet returned. His own evening had been a matter of killing time. Part of it he spent with Anita, and part with David and Freda.

Jim Harrington got up menacingly from his chair as Nigel entered the room. 'A fine couple of doctors you are,' he began to shout. 'Disgrace; that's what it is. But you're not going to get away with it this time.' A string of expletives followed. 'Doesn't matter a damn about your patients. That partner, or whatever you call him, gadding about, no doubt. No answer to the telephone, and his cottage in darkness.'

Nigel remained outwardly cold and calm

in the face of the abuse. Max was on duty and although Carolyn was with him, he would not have ignored both telephone and caller. A stab of jealousy, of fear, pierced him. Tormenting visions built up.

'What time was this?' he asked cautiously.

'What the hell do you care about time? Time in which my wife could have died.'

'Died.' Nigel felt slightly sick.

'Yes; no thanks to either of you that she's still alive – just.'

'Listen, Mr Harrington–'

'Listen, you say. *Listen.* I'm here to warn you, not to listen to any lies. The Disciplinary Committee of the Sussex Executive Council– Oh, yes, I've got my facts – will do the listening, and that'll bring you to heel. Max Faber. The excellent doctor, so you said. Well, we'll see about that.'

Nigel repeated his question. 'What time was this?'

'By phone from eight until nine. I went round after they'd got my wife to hospital.' He thumped his chest. 'I drove her there myself.'

'You – what?'

'Drove her there. What the hell else could I do? Your phone wasn't answered either. They couldn't refuse her in Casualty and they had to admit her. I tried Doctor Wren; he was delivering some damn baby.' There was hatred in the man's eyes as he added,

'Your house was in darkness when I got here... I'd have waited all night,' he added through half clenched teeth, so that the words seemed to be hissed out, instead of spoken.

'You say you went round to Dr Faber's cottage.'

'Are you doubting me? I went round; no lights in the place, but I banged and I thumped *and* I waited half an hour. If I know anything about doctors he was probably out with some blonde or other, while my wife – my *wife–*'

Nigel assessed him in that second. Tall; square shouldered, arrogant and belligerent. Over weight. His florid face was purple red with temper; his small eyes like blood-stained rapier points.

Nigel didn't underestimate his enemy, or overlook the justice of his case. It was obvious that Max and Carolyn had gone out together – forgetting everything except each other. He thought quickly. 'If you'll excuse me one second–' Abuse increased, but Nigel hurried out to Carolyn's room. *The telephone had not been switched through to Knoll Cottage.*

'Well?' Jim Harrington snapped as Nigel returned. 'Thought up some clever excuse.'

Nigel was very quiet as he said, 'I accept full responsibility for this. Doctor Faber is in no way to blame. A misunderstanding on my part.'

'And you have the damned nerve to stand there and admit it? No one to answer your telephone; no one in the blasted house at all, and you accept full responsibility. I'll say you accept it. And I'll tell you something else. I'm glad it's you I'm going to report and not Faber. Never did like you, but my wife did. Had to humour her. Now, you can take us off your list and be damned to you. This case won't do you any good in the neighbourhood. I'll see to that. Call yourself a doctor! Damned disgrace.' His face was distorted as spasms of temper shook him. He hated illness; he hated his wife being in hospital and his routine disorganised, and was thankful to be able to vent his anger – with just cause – on Nigel. He stormed out of the house and revved the car engine up as though on a racing track.

Nigel slumped in his chair. He was beyond thought. Only the sensations of misery and hurt were real.

Carolyn came into the house a matter of minutes later. She had hoped Nigel might be in bed, but the moment she saw him as he got up and stood with his back to the fire, she knew something was wrong. His gaze was cold and accusative.

'Did you enjoy your evening?'

'Very much. We had dinner at The White Hart.'

'I see. Without considering the fact that

Max was on call.'

She gave a little gasp and put her hand up to her mouth in a gesture of horror.

'Any more than you remembered to switch the telephone over to him.'

Her knees felt weak and she sat down in the nearest chair, shaking her head. Not only had she forgotten, but she had not given the practice a thought the whole evening. 'I'm so sorry.' Her voice broke. 'So sorry, Nigel.'

'So am I,' he said quietly. 'You see I've been out, too. Although you were with Max, it did not alter the fact that he was on duty.'

'And Mrs Mortimer—'

'Needless to say you also forgot that she had the evening off.'

'Yes.' Her eyes appealed to him. 'Everything was all right, though – wasn't it?'

He lit a cigarette. 'Unfortunately, no. Mrs Harrington was taken ill. I've had Harrington here. He'd tried to get Max; been to his cottage. I may detest the man, but he has right on his side. Two doctors; and neither available.' His pause was significant, 'But perhaps he has served a good purpose by bringing things to a head.' As he spoke, he turned towards her. 'Our life has become a farce, Carolyn, and I see no reason to perpetuate unhappiness rather than face facts.'

'I was going to talk to you,' she said, wretched because of the circumstances, and understanding how he must feel.

'I've known about you and Max – obviously. It's been pretty apparent.'

'Like your relationship with Anita.' Even in that second of tension she realised that all her rehearsed speeches were lost, the words empty of meaning. 'Have you seen her tonight?'

'Yes.'

'Will you marry her when you're free?'

Nigel felt that he had suddenly been thrown into icy water. How carefully she had thought it all out. He fought the jealousy that was like a knife in his heart; he fought the anger that made him want to accuse and condemn. Lowering his gaze to the fire, he said, 'Yes; so you see, it will suit us both.'

Carolyn had not expected this brief dismissal of their problems, while knowing that her own attitude had contributed to it. Now it seemed useless to ask questions, to discover more about Anita. Discussing the breakdown of their marriage would only lead to more antagonism. *It will suit us both* summed the situation up, thus removing any feeling of guilt on either side. For all that, woman-like, she wanted to know what had gone wrong, because Max was the effect and not the cause of this estrangement. She said a trifle defensively, 'One cannot live with secrets, Nigel.'

'And one cannot confide them where

there is no understanding.'

'One cannot give understanding to a block of ice.' Her eyes flashed him a fiery look.

'I see no point in discussing the past. It is enough to deal with the facts. And the present headache,' he added a trifle bitterly.

'Max will be reported.'

'Don't worry. I'll see he is well defended.' He could not bring himself to explain what he had done.

It wasn't what she meant; in fact, nothing was a true reflection of her thoughts, or feelings. Words tumbled out involuntarily. 'I'd like to think we could–'

'Remain good friends,' he cut in cynically, hurt goading him.

'Since we are agreed that this situation suits you as well as it does me, I don't see any justification for an injured air.'

'Perhaps it is a natural aversion to failure.' He studied her intently. She was still wearing her coat, as though she did not belong in the chair. Her face was pale and strained; yet she had never looked more beautiful, and he had never loved her so deeply. It was a savage, terrifying love that made it impossible for him to be helpful. Yet, contradictorily, the hurt in her eyes pained him. He wondered what would happen if he told her how he felt. For a second the impulse was overpowering. But the truth would make him her conscience and destroy some part of her happiness with Max. And while he hated Max, that was not the point at issue. His own life, his future, had been swirled into the melting pot. The idea of being at the mercy of Jim Harrington was distasteful, but not nearly so distasteful as having Max involved and, through him, Carolyn. The doctor having dinner with his partner's wife, when he ought to have been on duty ... he could imagine the scandal and gossip that would follow. The perfect bait for malicious tongues. The drama of a divorce case would be a nine days wonder, where this would hold all the suspense, the conjecture, of a lurid serial.

Carolyn's hands were clasped tightly in her lap. 'I feel dreadful. I can't *think* why I forgot the telephone.'

Nigel said more gently, 'Love has a knack of depriving us of memory.' His voice was flat as he added, 'Since you were not at the cottage all the time, it would not have made any difference.'

'You warned him against Mr Harrington.'

'Rather ironical that Harrington should be involved.'

The telephone rang and she gave a little fearful gasp.

'Speaking.' Nigel's face clouded. 'Been trying all the evening. I'm sorry... Vomiting and pain. I'll be over at once.'

Nigel said, as he dragged his coat on,

'Keep by the telephone. No; don't switch over to Max on any account. I'll be at the Mintons. Hope to heaven it isn't an appendix.'

The car raced from the house.

The Mintons, she thought anxiously. One of the lovely families. This emphasised the enormity of a doctor's responsibility. It was the first time that she had ever failed at her job. Throughout her training she had automatically reacted to discipline; cursing it, joking about it, but never falling down on the task at hand. And as a doctor's wife, she became the custodian of his reputation. She knew she had, until now, upheld it. She was wholly to blame, for neither Nigel, nor Max, could be expected to remember day to day arrangements. She had wanted to become their secretary, and quite apart from the domestic issue, no other consideration should have come into the scheme of things.

She shivered with fear as the telephone rang. 'Oh, yes, Mrs Andrews... Trying before?' Carolyn reacted quickly. 'The line has been engaged... Can I help you?'

'Well, I know it is very late, and that I ought to have got in touch with doctor before, but the baby is very flushed and crying. He won't go to sleep and hasn't eaten anything all day!' The voice rushed on, 'We can't settle down for the night, and my husband must have some rest. If we could be certain there is nothing wrong… As soon as he gets in. Thank you very much.'

Carolyn replaced the receiver, overwhelmingly relieved. In different circumstances there would have been an element of humour in the 'my husband must have some rest', since it was seldom assumed that the doctor required any. She sat by the dying fire, sick at heart. For the evening to have ended on this note brought a feeling of bereavement.

Nigel returned just before midnight and immediately went off again. 'Don't wait up,' he said shortly, 'the telephone is by your bed, so there's no point in your sitting down here.'

'Nigel–'

'Yes.' He looked back at her from the door.

'Only that Max wanted to talk to you tonight. There was no question of his just leaving things to me.'

Nigel nodded. The front door shut.

18

When Max arrived at Downs Cottage the following morning, Nigel had already left on his rounds.

Carolyn looked strained, and not even discreet make-up could conceal the fact. Max looked at her with questioning anxiety.

'You were on call last night,' she said, her voice low. 'And I forgot to switch the telephone over.'

Max stared at her and cried in a breath, 'My God! Of course I was. It went out of my head.'

'And mine.'

'Oh, *Carolyn* ... I said *out of my head*. I suppose that's true, but had I stopped to think... Trouble?'

'Mr Harrington. You see, Nigel was out also.'

'That means,' said Max, 'I'll be hauled up before the executive council.' He paled.

'I'm to blame,' she insisted. 'I didn't even think of the telephone. I suppose I must have been in the state of mind to assume, at least sub-consciously, that Nigel would be here.'

'What was his attitude?'

'Everything came at once... You see, Harrington had just left him when I returned. It brought things to a head.'

'You told him about us?' Max was watching every shade of expression on her face.

Carolyn drew a hand across her forehead. 'It wasn't so much a question of telling him, as his telling me.' She outlined all that had been said and when she had finished, Max was suddenly very quiet, then, 'So he and Anita... It's true. I'm glad. That makes me feel better... Do you regret my coming into your life?'

Carolyn raised her gaze to his. 'Can one regret being brought back to life? I'm just worried about you. It is the last thing one wanted just now.'

'Harrington has a case – a genuine grievance. I couldn't deny it. I can only place the facts before the Medical Defence Union. Obviously Nigel does not come into this.'

'But,' Carolyn persisted, 'I had forgotten to switch the telephone over to you, so that in any case–'

Max cut in firmly, 'That will not be put forward in any evidence. I shall not be reported because of where I was, or with whom. I shall be faced with negligence and not being available while on duty. This is where I'll have to take my own medicine,' he finished with an attempt at humour.

Carolyn looked as depressed as she felt.

'Mrs Harrington has always been well looked after – far beyond normal limits.'

'Beyond terms of service,' Max said with a touch of bitterness.

'I feel so guilty... Personal matters don't change that. You are associated with Nigel, and it was my job to protect you both.'

Max did not betray the fear that was making him feel sick. This was a blow striking far deeper than Carolyn knew. It held an irony which only Nigel would understand.

The silence that fell held no comfort.

'You will forget all about that,' he exclaimed, and his expression held a note of warning. 'Now ... work. I'll talk to Nigel later on. We both want to know where we stand, and our plans for the immediate future. Divorce, in cases like ours, needs to be carefully handled.'

Divorce. It sounded a foreign word just then, Carolyn thought. The harsh light of day was vastly different from the candlelight of the previous night. Then, there had been a richness, a mellowness; now an emptiness linked up with uncertainty and apprehension. She felt rather like a cardboard figure as she went into the hall to greet Max's first patient – a Mrs Cavendish, glowing and eager with anticipation, hoping to have her first pregnancy confirmed. To Carolyn she looked so much younger than her twenty-one years. Or was it that she, herself, felt so much older than usual?

'I'm so excited,' Mrs Cavendish confided, a little shyly, as Carolyn took her into the examining room. 'You see, we planned the baby. I always said I wanted a baby when I was twenty-one.'

'A lovely twenty-first birthday present,' Carolyn suggested.

The fair head nodded. 'I was married when I was nineteen ... but you know all about me. Doctor Faber is very nice, isn't he? We all like him.'

'I'm glad.' Carolyn felt very isolated. The shining, carefree happiness on the face of this girl emphasised her own position.

'It's so nice having you here, Mrs Blake. You understand and don't make me feel stupid, or awkward.'

'I should hope not... Comfortable?'

'Yes; beautifully warm.'

Carolyn wished she could lie there, secure and relaxed and drift off into blissful sleep. A feeling of shame weighed upon her because of all that had happened. It tarnished everything that, previously, had seemed straightforward. She went into Max's consulting room.

'Ready?'

'Yes.'

As he passed her he picked up her hand and kissed it. 'Don't worry, darling,' he whispered gently. 'It isn't the end of the world.'

She gave him a tremulous smile. When she saw him again, Mrs Cavendish had gone. 'No doubt about that one,' he said cheerfully, and then added, 'Sorry I shan't be around to deliver her, but I couldn't tell her so – not at this stage.'

Carolyn started. 'But–'

'There are plenty more babies to be delivered, in every part of the country – or the world,' he added quietly.

Nigel came in and the three of them looked at each other in a tense, wary silence before Nigel said, 'I suggest we discuss all the problems tomorrow evening.' His voice held a note of authority. 'I've got that long report to send off on Mrs Minton. She must be seen by Norman Candell.'

'You want me to make an appointment?' Carolyn asked.

'Friday, if possible. He's always frantically busy, but his secretary is pretty good at fitting in my patients.'

'Yes, I know.' How easily he was able to brush aside all personal issues, even to the point of talking as though she were not associated with his work. In truth, Nigel wanted to know exactly where he stood with Anita, taking into account the present circumstances, before he entered into any detailed discussion regarding the future. Uppermost in his mind was the desire that Carolyn should be happy, and given her freedom at no matter what cost to himself. To dwell on the unbearability of his own loss was agonising, but not nearly so agonising as it would be to continue living with her, knowing that she was in love with Max. Even so, he wanted to accustom himself to the first deadly awareness of a life crumbling around him. It was like taking an analgesic for a permanent headache, clinging to the ridiculous hope that the pain might vanish.

He began dictating without making any further comment, sitting back in his chair, swivelling it round so that he avoided watching Carolyn's solemn face, and trying not to allow his mind to wander.

'I'm sorry,' she said apologetically, 'I missed the last sentence.'

He repeated it, and when the task was finished, she went into her room and made the call to London.

'Mr Candell can see Mrs Minton on Friday at five,' she said as she returned.

'Good. What is the appointment book like on Friday?'

'Easy, after hospital.'

'Max can take over. I may make a weekend of it.' He got up from his chair. 'And I shan't be in after surgery this evening... If you'd get that typed, I'd be grateful. It can go off with the day's post then.'

'Very well... How was the Andrews' baby last night?'

'Colic.' He looked at her for the first time and then went from the room. The monosyllable was not abrupt, merely a statement of fact to which he had nothing he wished to add. He saw Max a little later on in the day, and managed to speak to him while they were alone. 'I'll be over at the cottage later on tonight. There are things you and I must get straight between us.'

They faced each other with veiled hostility.

'Very well,' Max agreed.

'And make certain the telephone is switched through.' The words were a reminder, uttered without trace of emotion. 'If you should be out on a call, I'll wait in my car.'

'I understand.'

Max left the house immediately after seeing his last patient out, and while Nigel was still engaged with his. Carolyn had a dazed expression in her eyes as Max said, 'Unless I'm called out I'll be at the cottage from now on. Switch over to me when Nigel leaves the house.'

Carolyn went into the sitting-room and sank down in her chair, weary to the point of exhaustion and tears.

Mrs Mortimer came in.

'I'll be alone this evening,' Carolyn forced a smile. 'I'd like something light.'

'An omelette, perhaps?'

'A good idea.' Actually the thought was revolting. 'I'll have it on a tray in here.'

'Anything for doctor when he gets back?' Mrs Mortimer could not bear the sadness and apprehension in Carolyn's eyes.

'No thank you. He will probably be late.' Carolyn shivered. 'I'm awfully cold.'

Mrs Mortimer piled a few more logs on the fire. They blazed in what was now an unhappy house; a house dark with shadows. 'That's better,' she said.

Carolyn heard the door of Max's car slam and felt a tremor of fear. Why had he returned? 'I went without my bag,' he explained, and hesitated while Mrs Mortimer left them. 'What are you going to do this evening?'

'Try to eat an omelette and go to bed early.'

'I hate leaving you.' His voice was husky. 'Think of last night – nothing can take those hours away.'

She forced a smile.

'And don't worry about Harrington. Doctors are always being hauled over the coals for something.' His tone changed. 'I'm not overlooking Nigel's point of view. As his assistant-cum-partner I represent him, and I couldn't have fallen down on my job for a worse reason. He could never be expected to look at it in any other way.'

'If – if Mrs Harrington were to die?'

'Obviously it would make things more grim. But it is my guess that a spell in hospital, away from household worries, may be her salvation.'

Nothing anyone said could take away Carolyn's feeling of guilt.

19

'I think,' Anita said, 'we had better eat.'

'Food.' Nigel uttered the word with distaste, adding hastily, 'You mean you have prepared something?'

'Yes; your voice over the telephone didn't sound as though you were in the mood for having dinner out.'

He gave a half smile. 'Bad as that?'

'Yes. A drink?'

'Ah!' His sigh was deep as he sat down, and then took the glass she offered him. It struck him that here was a different world and that, while Anita was a member of his profession, her home escaped any sign of the fact. There was nothing about it he could fault, but it seemed like a perfect set on the stage because of its unfamiliarity. Yet he had been there on several occasions. This was different; he was seeing it through the eyes of a man about to tear up his roots, give up one habit and try to adapt himself to another. The familiar phrase that habit was stronger than emotion had never rung more true, although he could have added, contradictorily, that the two could be one and the same thing. Now that he was there he found it extremely difficult to say what was in his mind. The whole thing seemed an impertinence, and his conceit overwhelming. As against that, he had either to believe all that Anita had previously told him about her feelings for him, or not.

Anita watched him carefully; her heart beats were uneven. It was impossible for her to be in his presence without an upsurge of emotion and excitement. Now she held her breath, his changing expressions filling her with suspense.

'Suppose,' she said at last, 'you come to the point, Nigel. Whatever it is I shall not be offended.' Even as she spoke she had a recurrence of the feeling that she was two people; the one selfish and scheming, the other capable of great love and, if necessary, sacrifice.

Nigel got up from his chair as though incapable of making any statement while sitting down. She waited patiently while he paced the floor a few times, then willed his gaze to meet hers. He flopped back into the chair, leaned forward, his elbows on his knees, and said with startling directness, 'I want to give Carolyn grounds for divorce. Would you be willing to be co-respondent in the action?'

Anita could not have said what she had expected, but certainly not that startling question. She managed to keep all emotion from her voice as she asked, 'Meaning that my services end with the evidence?'

Nigel gasped, 'Good lord, no. Of course I want you to marry me.'

'Marry you,' she echoed disbelievingly.

Nigel sat back in his chair and gulped the remainder of his whisky.

'Yes,' he repeated, 'marry me.'

A little sick sensation struck at the pit of her stomach; tears were very near her eyes. 'All this for Carolyn's happiness – and protection.'

His gaze did not swerve from hers. 'Yes,' he admitted honestly. 'At least in the sense that you mean, but it goes far beyond that.'

'You still love her, don't you?'

'Yes.' He lit a cigarette. 'Even so, I couldn't go on. It isn't just Max. Somewhere, we lost our way. God knows where. My fault, perhaps. It does not matter.'

'Have you any love for me, Nigel?'

'A very great deal. Enough to ask you this – this outrageous question,' he added sincerely.

A heavy silence fell between them. Anita tried to catch some thread from the past and weave it into the pattern of the moment. *Co-respondent.* It was curious that previously, and at any time, she would have gone to bed with him without thinking beyond the ecstasy of being in his arms; now, the cold calculation of such an act, interpreted in a

256

single word, demanded courage momentarily beyond her. Her hesitation made him say, 'Anita, forgive my clumsiness and–'

She interrupted, her resolve strengthening. 'There is nothing to forgive. My answer is yes. Just for a moment I suppose I could not grasp it all.'

'Small wonder. I can't quite grasp it myself. But any other way would seem wrong.'

'Meaning that you would be prepared to allow her to divorce you in any case?'

'Yes.'

'What irony... Your turning to me. Perhaps my coming here will have proved right after all.'

'You realise that the situation is not going to be easy? In our profession there is no such thing as sliding out and avoiding publicity. Your career, for instance.'

'If I had to choose between that and being your wife – no matter what the circumstances – I should not have to think twice. I am not your patient, so we shall not be at the mercy of the G.M.C. Doctors have been divorced before, and will be again.'

'I shall do my best to keep your name out of it,' he said firmly. 'And I am quite certain that Carolyn will co-operate as far as possible in order to get her freedom.' The pain and the bitterness of love gave an edge of cynicism to his words.

'When I came over to dinner that night, I

257

found Carolyn different, somehow. Her feelings for Max making her kind. There wasn't any jealousy of me.' Anita put down her sherry glass. 'You were foolish not to have told her everything.'

'I know that. All reasons are valid at the time. Afterwards, understanding has gone.' As he spoke his heart felt like a stone, and as cold. Nothing was real.

They had dinner in the small candle-lit dining-room. The round table was artistically set and the silver gleamed. But all the time Nigel's thoughts of Carolyn were visual. Through the mellow light he saw – as though it were superimposed on the scene – the blazing fire in the sitting-room at Downs Cottage, and the two strangers who had recently sat beside it – strangers who had no point of contact and whose disharmony made any kind of communication impossible. The ghost of Max haunted him. Max loving her, kissing her...

'Will you forgive me?' Nigel's knife and fork went down on his plate, the cold chicken hardly touched.

Anita rested her hand on his, the gesture full of understanding. 'I can't eat any more either. I'll make some coffee.'

They went back to their comfortable chairs.

Nigel drank his coffee in silence for a few seconds. 'Strange how words have a knack of creating situations that are entirely false, and yet lies do not come into it.'

'Meaning?' Anita looked puzzled.

'Carolyn merely asked me if I should marry you. It wasn't necessary for me to enlarge on anything. All I said was, yes.'

Anita studied him reflectively. 'Why is it you so seldom explain anything, or talk about your feelings?'

He looked surprised. 'I wasn't aware of being like that. I certainly hate ten words where one would do.'

'Sometimes ten are needed to qualify one.'

He looked confused. 'Perhaps recently I've avoided any topic that might stimulate questioning.'

'A fatal thing. Also, you appear to be so absent-minded that I doubt if you hear half of what is being said to you.'

'Don't make me sound too boring.'

She looked at him very levelly. 'I don't expect pretty speeches–'

He cut in rather sharply, the recollection of that phrase stinging him. 'And I'd hate having to make them... Sorry, Anita. That makes me an unutterable bore. When all this is over, we'll go right away. Out of the country for a real holiday, and I'll be human again. I'm not exactly poor.'

'That makes two of us,' she exclaimed.

Memory swirled Nigel back to the night when he told Carolyn he could not go on as he was, and her reply had been, 'That makes two of us'. Obviously, she was tired of life with him even then. Her discontent and desire to work actively in the practice – everything tied up. Max had arrived in her life at exactly the right moment.

'I could never live at Downs Cottage,' Anita said firmly. 'You would understand that – wouldn't you?'

'Perfectly. There are plenty of other houses in the district, should we decide to remain there.' His expression was unyielding. 'I'm sure that Carolyn will not want to stay, and Max will move on to another appointment.'

Anita said breathlessly, 'We could work together in partnership, Nigel.'

It was a reasonable statement, but it struck a chill at his heart. In a very different way he and Carolyn had worked together, and although not in the happiest, or most favourable, circumstances nevertheless the practice had been a bond between them.

'We shall have to be guided by events,' he said trying not to be evasive.

She made no comment, but her expression was sympathetic. A little later she stood at the window and watched him walk to his car. He looked up at her before sliding into the driving seat. She waited until the rear light disappeared as he turned on to the sea front.

The room was still filled with his presence

as she sat down and tried to curb the excitement and overwhelming happiness that made life glow. It did not matter, at this stage, that he was not in love with her. She argued that time was on her side, and his need of her would create an emotion in itself. She would not be the cause of the upheaval in his marriage, therefore no antagonism could be roused because of her guilt. What was more, he would have proof of her loyalty and readiness to risk all the social disadvantages, even a possible adverse effect upon her career itself. And while he might argue that she was getting everything on which she had set her heart, it was certainly not being achieved in triumph. Nigel's *wife*. No price was too great to pay for the privilege – not even living with Carolyn's ghost for a while...

Nigel drove back along the familiar Brighton-Lewes Road without actually seeing a landmark. His thoughts were like ghosts creeping out of the darkness and surrounding him in a strange world of hideous fantasy. His visit to Anita had been a projection of that fantasy. Now, enclosed in his car, he felt a stranger to himself; a figure travelling in the wrong direction, and at the wrong speed. Even his own name was alien; his profession associated only with the man who qualified many years before; the man who bore no resemblance to the doctor living at Downs Cottage. That, too, ceased to be home, and was a house to which he would return later that night, as he might return to a hotel bedroom.

Max let him in without any greeting, beyond asking him if would have a drink, the mere possession of a glass breaking a little of the tension and cutting across formality. They sat down, and in the mind of both was a picture of other evenings when they had talked far into the night, the bond of friendship strong and unshakable.

'Just how sincere are you Max? How deep is your regard for Carolyn. It is useless evading the issue. I want the truth.'

Max looked at him fearlessly. 'Carolyn means more to me than anything else in life. The thing I hate most is the fact that she happens to be married to you. I'm not going to attempt to make any excuses. You're not the type to tolerate them, anyway.'

Nigel's voice deepened. 'If you hurt her I think I'd be capable of murder.'

Max was shocked by the warning note, and Nigel's grim expression.

'And I think, in those circumstances, you would be justified. It's not easy to face a man and tell him that one is very much in love with his wife, but that is precisely what I am doing.'

Nigel tried not to allow emotion, jealousy and crushing regret, to fire the conversation with anger, or animosity.

'Then I must take your word.'

'You can also take it that nothing has happened between Carolyn and me, except the realisation of how we feel.'

'I believe that.'

'And since your marriage has been in name only – at least for some time – I'd be a hypocrite to see all this in terms of tragedy. You have Anita and–' He made a gesture with his hand to convey that no harm would be done.

The words 'in name only' cut into Nigel's heart like a dagger. It was a truth he found hardest to bear. He had no intention of discussing his relationship with Anita, or enlarging on what Max had said.

An uncomfortable silence fell between them, and then Nigel exclaimed, 'There is just one thing I must ask you.'

Max tensed. 'Such as?'

'I've had a suspicion that you were the man in the Moreen Fuller case. Was I right?'

'Quite right.' Max lowered his gaze and then said quietly, 'I told Carolyn some part of the story, and she guessed who it was. There is nothing else in the past for her ever to know.' He looked at Nigel very directly. 'I'm sure you will agree with that.'

'Thank you, yes. We do not want confusion and complications.'

Max held out his cigarette case and Nigel

took a cigarette. Max knew that there could never be real enmity between them. They might dislike each other now, but that dislike could not embrace either revenge or malice, but merely the natural aversion between two men involved with one woman. He made allowances for the fact that, while Nigel was in love with Anita, it did not preclude him from retaining affection for Carolyn.

For both of them it was like sitting back and watching transparencies projected on the screen of years, aware how closely their lives had been linked.

'I shall not forget your taking me into the practice,' Max said suddenly. 'Neither shall I cease to be grateful. If I seem to have repaid you in a rather poor fashion, then I must accept that condemnation as justified. Never having really loved before… What made you link me with Moreen Fuller?' He spoke as though the truth had only just sunk in.

'Several things; the first day you saw her at Downs Cottage. I suggested that you needed the brandy, and her sudden decision to have the child adopted. Also your manner when I mentioned the accident.'

'I remember. Nothing will ever make me less of a cad than I was over that. Frightening to be able to stick pins in oneself.'

Nigel bristled, 'It was a damnable case, but if Carolyn is satisfied with your story–'

'She is satisfied with the truth.' Max's

temper flared. 'You have yet to doubt that, Nigel.'

Nigel apologised. For that moment, emotion whipped up anger. How deeply Carolyn must be in love in order to accept the situation. Depression seeped into him like a cold clammy fog... Carolyn had been in this room... His gaze focussed the sofa. No doubt they had both sat there together, planning for the future, and wondering how best to break the news to *him*.

'That brings me to the Harrington case.' Nigel lit a cigarette as he spoke, trying to calm his nerves.

'I've no excuse for that, either, and no defence. One thing I can assure you, Carolyn will not come into it, and no mention will be made of the telephone.'

Nigel said firmly, 'In this, Max, you will do exactly as I say. Let's cut out our personal and domestic problems, and deal just with Harrington. I have already told him that I take full responsibility and that the fault was mine.'

'You've done – what?'

'I don't have to repeat it.'

'And do you seriously think–'

Nigel cut in with, 'There is no question of thinking. The matter is settled. I don't want you mixed up in it. No one could guarantee, in the circumstances, that your movements that night would not be suspect, and that

Carolyn's name could be safeguarded.'

The room seemed so quiet that even the ticking of the clock was lost in the silence. Max burst out, 'You cannot force me to agree. Carolyn need not come into it, as I said.'

'That may well be, but I am not taking any chances. What is more, I have a long memory.'

'Good God, Nigel, this is different—'

'How? Harrington is delighted to be able to have a go at me, and openly admitted that he was glad you were not at fault. He'll build up all his expenses so that I'm fined as well as reprimanded. Obviously, I'll hand the case over to the Medical Defence Union and that will be that. I'll have to appear, but I've made my decision.' He added quietly, 'There is always poetic justice.'

'That doesn't make me hate it any the less.'

'I've one last thing to ask of you.'

'What?' There was no compromise in Max's voice.

'No word of this to Carolyn.'

'But she's bound to find out.'

'Not necessarily. The patients like her too well to bring up the subject, even if they know about it. I told her I would do all I could to help you. What is more, they can delve as much as they damn well like into my affairs... If you get my meaning.'

'I hadn't thought of that,' Max sighed as he spoke.

'It was my first thought,' Nigel hastened. 'Also it would be very fishy if you attempted to take the blame now that Harrington has his teeth into me. He's an unpleasant customer, and mud slinging would give him enormous satisfaction. He's got a bona fide case, but that's all the satisfaction he can get as things stand now.'

'I shall refund any fine you pay!' Max insisted.

'That isn't important, and I have your word as far as Carolyn is concerned?'

Max shook his head. 'You're a strange man, Nigel. You'd go to any lengths to spare her – even in these circumstances – and yet you refuse to allow her to give you one iota of credit.'

Nigel met Max's eyes, his own direct and challenging. 'Haven't you worked on those lines? I don't overlook anything. This way, all that has to be done is to let Carolyn know that Harrington is not reporting you. That will be true.'

'It is a fantastic situation,' Max hesitated. 'Coming back to other things. Do you want me to get out of the practice immediately?'

Nigel looked grave. 'No; that would be unwise and start unnecessary conjecture. At the end of six months – not all that long now – you will be able to leave the district without any complications. It will also enable you and Carolyn to make your plans. After that, she can divorce me.'

Max looked startled.

'You and Carolyn are not guilty,' Nigel explained resolutely, prepared for Max to assume that he and Anita were. 'Don't worry, it will all be a nine days wonder. The patients love a little scandal. The shocked are invariably jealous and frustrated; the tolerant, indifferent; and the malicious always have the knack of becoming such bores that they rally opinion to the other side!' Nigel felt that every word he was uttering was out of character and meaningless. Futility weighed upon him; there was no escape from a deadly reality. The ringing of the telephone came almost as a relief.

Max reached out from his chair. 'Freda. Last night… What can I do for you? No, I shouldn't curse if I were "dragged" out as you call it. Cocktail party? I'd like to. Next Wednesday.' The receiver went back on its cradle.

Nigel said, 'We're going.' He stopped; the *we* had significance. 'These are the invitations we cannot avoid – you too – at the moment. It struck me just then that you might consider taking over my list and carrying on the practice, should I decide to leave England. It could be the answer. Your marrying Carolyn, at some discreet distant date, would please the romantics,' he added cynically. 'You wouldn't need to keep the practice at Downs Cottage. It's the doctor that matters – not the house.'

Max gave no definite answer. He was too amazed by the trend of the conversation, and Nigel's attitude in general.

At the door, on his way out, Nigel said, 'So far as Harrington is concerned, I'll let you know the moment I hear from the executive council. You will have to take over the work while I go up to discuss the whole thing with the Union. Carolyn will assume I am with Anita, so that will not present any problem.'

Max nodded and then asked abruptly, 'By the way, why didn't you mention Moreen Fuller before?'

'Because I was not the custodian of your morals – at least not until tonight.'

'I'm grateful to have been able to talk to Carolyn myself before now.'

Nigel had already stepped out into the moonlit darkness. 'I should not have told her – even had I been given proof – but I should have insisted on your doing so.'

Max returned to the fire after Nigel's car had driven away. He tried to shut out the ghosts, and the visions, hardly daring to dwell on the happiness to come.

20

Carolyn felt that she was living without a roof over her head during the days that followed. The house was there; she was in it, but like someone thrust into outer space. Nigel treated her with polite consideration which she could not fault.

'Would you prefer that I got someone else in to take over the practice work?' He managed to talk without looking at her for longer than a few seconds.'

'No,' she said firmly. 'The general situation doesn't alter my liking for my job.'

'And it does enable you to see Max with perfect justification.' He tried to keep the chagrin from his voice.

She raised her head slightly. 'Hove is a convenient distance away, also, and not a country area. You are not in the least handicapped.'

'I'm sorry,' came the terse comment, 'to have the momentary advantage; yours will come when you can divorce me.'

Were he and Anita already lovers? Even to pose the question made her seem naïve.

'That will be a mutual advantage. I've never associated the word with divorce before.'

'Divorce is a word rather like murder – always associated with the other person's life, never one's own. Unfortunately, doctors have far greater responsibilities than the rest of the community. Their homes require careful putting in order before they can, contradictorily, be smashed up. But there is no need to be anxious because we are sharing this house. Mrs Mortimer and Mrs Pringle can vouch for the fact that, for some time, ours has been a marriage in name only. There is no question of collusion. When I leave, these details will substantiate your evidence and absolve you absolutely. On the other hand, if you would rather move out for a while – a convenient holiday somewhere – you have only to say.'

Carolyn found that she could neither think nor speak. The wreckage around her was numbing; a wreckage of hopes, ideals, illusions and, quite unexpectedly, the hurt of it all tore at her. Nigel's voice had an inexorable quality.

'Well?'

Carolyn said quietly, 'Seeing that you can stand it here, so can I.'

'It is at least an original situation.' He looked up his appointments book and said, 'By the way, Glenda Phillips' husband died this morning. He was drunk and wrapped his car round a lamp standard. They really believed he was cured this time. At least now she will be spared further misery and suspense.' He looked at his watch without noticing the time. 'Death can sometimes be kinder than heart-ache. Grief is not a conflict. He was brought into casualty while I was at the hospital. I saw her and broke the news.'

'How is she?'

Nigel sighed and got to his feet. 'Shocked; brave. I hope there is happiness for her somewhere. She mentioned you, remembering your kindness that night when she lost the child.'

They looked at each other sharing the remembrance. It seemed yesterday, and a thousand years ago. She had often read of people being divorced and yet condemned to live in the same house, because of the housing shortage. She and Nigel might have already been divorced for, without antagonism, they managed adroitly to avoid each other. Work had become an impersonal task, carried out as an efficient routine. Discussions were not indulged in. No questions were asked. Not even the presence of Max destroyed the cool detachment which enabled them to behave like two people living in an hotel, exchanging commonplaces. The reference to Glenda Philips plunged Carolyn back into a mood of depression she could neither combat nor explain.

Nigel went on quickly, 'No doubt Max has

told you that Harrington isn't reporting him.'

Carolyn's eyes held both surprise and overwhelming relief. 'No,' she cried.

'He will tell you when he comes in. That's one worry off your mind. I'm very thankful.'

She forced him to meet her questioning eyes. 'Did you persuade Mr Harrington?'

Nigel shook his head. 'No. Any approach from me would have done Max a disservice.'

'Your attitude has been very generous.'

'Not really. Everything in life is a matter of "there but for the grace of God".'

Carolyn sat down beside the desk, slightly faint. Her nerves tingled; relief overwhelmed her. 'I've been very worried.'

'I know.' Nigel had considered it tactful to wait a few days before mentioning the matter. A man like Harrington changing his mind overnight would have aroused suspicion. It brought home to Nigel just how deeply concerned Carolyn had been for Max. No communication had come from the executive council so far as he, himself, was concerned, but he did not expect to receive it for some days.

The telephone rang and Carolyn answered it. 'Yes, Anita... One moment.' She handed Nigel the receiver and went out of the consulting room.

'Why,' she asked Max a little later, 'didn't

you tell me about Mr Harrington and the case?' She did not realise that her voice held reproach.

'This would have been my first opportunity,' he replied. It was previously arranged that Nigel should mention the fact.

'Oh! I've been so worried. One never knows with these things.'

Max felt embarrassed and handicapped.

'This,' he said evasively, 'isn't exactly a pleasant time for any of us. Nigel has certainly taken it in his stride.'

Carolyn felt irritated. 'Anita telephoned just now. I suppose you'd say that she is happy enough to sound charming.'

'Then I must sound like that, too.' He watched Carolyn carefully.

'You have always been charming.'

Max smiled. 'I wish I could whisk you away at this moment, without all the problems and practice details to settle.'

She said involuntarily, 'I want to get away from here, Max. Right away.' Her gaze travelled around the sitting-room. 'I don't believe in taking the past into the future.'

'No,' Max agreed, 'neither do I.'

'What Nigel decides about the practice is his affair, after all. He is only answerable to the N.H.S.' Faint cynicism tinged her voice. 'Pity that he and Anita cannot join forces and run it together. I doubt if anyone would object, once they are respectably married.'

Max said, 'That sounds bitter.'

Faint colour tinged her cheeks. 'Just that convention–' She stopped.

'Nigel can hardly do more than allow *you* to divorce *him.*' Max chose his words carefully.

'We could not provide him with evidence.'

'Would you rather it were done that way?' Max moved nearer to her and put his hands on her shoulders. 'Would you, Carolyn?'

'In some ways I suppose I would. He could stay here, then, and keep the practice as it is. After all, this is his home and his career has been built around it. Who has, or who has not, been unfaithful isn't really what matters most. The four of us are in the same boat.' She hesitated.

'What is it?' Max looked into her troubled eyes. He held her close for a second and then moved away.

'The confusion of not knowing what is right, or wrong. How best to simplify things.'

Max lit a cigarette. 'If you feel like this I could talk to him.'

She shook her head. 'You can't *talk* to Nigel. He's made the decisions before you start.'

'His decisions are not unfair, all the same.'

She looked ashamed. 'I know.'

Max glanced at his watch. A patient was due in a matter of minutes.

'He would get enormous sympathy and

support if I ran off with you the moment I'd finished here. I'm more than willing to do it that way – if you are.' Max argued that, in this, Nigel's wishes were not of paramount importance, despite what had been said between them.

Mrs Mortimer brought in some coffee, putting the tray down and saying, 'I thought you might like this before the bell rings.'

'She is a remarkable woman,' Max exclaimed, as the door shut. 'Aware of everything; conveying nothing except pleasantness...'

'She would stay on with Nigel,' Carolyn murmured reflectively. 'Keep everything the same. I can't bear the idea of her going.' She drank a little coffee. 'Amazing all the things that come into the breaking up of a home.'

'Life demands its price for everything.'

A sick sensation settled in Carolyn's stomach, which felt empty and churned up. There was a lump in her throat and she swallowed hard. She would miss Mrs Mortimer and Mrs Pringle; they had become part of her life.

And in the kitchen, drinking their coffee, Mrs Pringle said, 'I hear Mr Harrington's flinging his weight about. Boasting about how hot he will make things for Doctor... I just listen.'

'Just keep listening, Mrs Pringle; you can't be had up for that.'

'Things don't get better.'

Mrs Mortimer lowered her head and stared down at the plate on which she had set out a few biscuits. 'No; they don't get better. Mrs Blake isn't well, either.'

'What do you think is going to happen?'

'I wish I knew,' said Mrs Mortimer sadly. 'I feel that everything I do may be for the last time.'

'They'd never get rid of us without fair warning,' Mrs Pringle exclaimed stoutly. 'Never.'

'I'm sure of that. All we can do is to carry on and pretend not to notice anything.'

'Doctor Faber never stays for any meals now.'

'Less washing up,' said Mrs Mortimer briskly, trying to cheer herself up. She got to her feet; the session was over. She could not understand Doctor Blake. It wasn't that he treated her any differently, but he no longer seemed to belong in the house. Also, there was the business over the letters. He had taken to coming down early and going through them. It was very mysterious, but she was not paid to solve mysteries. All the same, it was obvious there was some communication he wished to keep from Mrs Blake.

Nigel heard from the executive council about a week later. A complaint had been made by Mr Harrington. He read it almost with relief. Now there was no question about Harrington being persuaded by his wife not to proceed with the matter. It had been a fugitive hope, but he knew that Mrs Harrington would be the first to appreciate the fact that he had given her meticulous care over a considerable period of time.

'And that care,' he said to Max later on in the morning, 'will at least stand to my credit with the Union, even though I have no defence against the actual complaint.'

'I detest this,' Max said with vehemence.

'I'll go up to the Union tomorrow,' Nigel went on, as though Max had not spoken.

Carolyn asked no questions when Nigel announced his intention of going to London. All she said was, 'I shall ask Freda over.'

'I shan't be back for dinner.'

'I'm afraid I can't quite see the connection.'

'Only if David should collect her and stay.'

'That is unlikely, and since she will come over in her own car – unnecessary. In any case, foursomes are a thing of the past. We shall have to tell them the situation.'

'Of course. The vital thing is to devise a plan to serve the practice best. There are certain things I have to settle. It won't be long before the strain is over for us both.' He looked at her and then quickly lowered his gaze. 'You have my calls listed for Max?'

'Yes.' She noticed he was wearing his black jacket and pin-striped trousers. He looked both smart and professional. His tall, slim figure set off whatever clothes he happened to favour, and his clean-cut features were enhanced by the whiteness of his collar which also emphasised his tan – a tan he managed to retain, even in winter. Was he visiting a patient? It was obvious that he would be meeting Anita, if not travelling up with her. It was reasonable to assume that he had to fit in his time with hers. Even in these circumstances, he usually gave Max longer notice before turning over all his work to him. She watched him leave the house and get into his car, but there was no question of seeing him off, or going to the door. Looking through his consulting room window she found it incredible to think that he was her husband; that they had shared a life together; laughed, been gay, sad, argumentative – all the normal expressions of marriage, which included an exchange of ideas, and planning for the future.

Max came and stood behind her, following her gaze. He bent and kissed the nape of her neck in a swift adoring gesture. 'I love you,' he whispered softly, and hurried back to his own room as he heard the door bell ring, knowing it would be a patient.

Freda came over that afternoon. Carolyn felt awkward, even shy, as she greeted her and they sat down over the fire together. She wanted to confide in her, but shrank from discussions. It wasn't that she feared Freda's criticism (Freda was not the type to disparage, or condemn, anyone) but there was so much conflict in her own mind that it would seem like telling only half a story. She envied Freda the carefree happiness so obvious in her radiant face. It was like standing outside a lighted window looking in on a party to which she had not been invited. They talked fitfully with slight uneasy pauses interspersing the conversation until, at last, Freda said, her expression gentle and sympathetic, 'We're so sorry about that wretched man, Harrington.'

Carolyn tensed as she met Freda's gaze. She said cautiously, suspense making her heart beat unevenly, 'He always has been a trouble maker.'

'But to go for Nigel, of *all* people. I just want you to know how David and I feel.'

Carolyn managed to keep her voice steady as she asked, 'You mean that Mr Harrington is–?' She stopped, as a wave of faintness went over her.

'Broadcasting his grievance, and boasting how watertight his case is. He won't make any impression on Nigel's patients, but I'd like to get a hammer to the man. The most unpleasant, bad-tempered bore who ever lived. David's come up against him. Why he should have a grudge against Nigel is beyond me.' Freda stopped, realising how pale Carolyn looked. Consternation spread over her face. 'I haven't told you anything you didn't know?' she said, appalled by the thought.

'Can you imagine gossip escaping me?'

Freda's body sagged with relief. 'Just for one awful moment I thought I'd made one of my best clangers.'

'Oh, no,' Carolyn assured her. 'Dear Mr Harrington honoured us with a visit.'

'I hope he chokes. Is Nigel very upset?'

'Irritated. No doctor likes to be hauled up and reprimanded for any negligence or breach of service.' Carolyn felt that she was going down in a bumpy lift. It was obvious that Nigel had deceived her about the case and was protecting Max. Was this for *her* sake, or his own? And if for her sake, why could he not have told her? It wasn't possible that Max had forced his hand. Her thoughts scuttled back to Christmas Eve when she had overheard Max saying to Nigel, 'You've no need to fear that I shall say anything.'

Freda, sensitive to Carolyn's moods – as opposed to moodiness – knew instinctively that, quite apart from the Harrington business, something was radically wrong at Downs Cottage. The atmosphere was full of unrest, as it had been to a lesser degree even before Max Faber's advent. She could not help wondering where Anita fitted into the picture. There was suffering stamped on Carolyn's face, and she smiled only with her lips, not her eyes. Everything was dull, empty and flat. Conversation that once had sparkled was now disjointed and without any confidential note. She knew that Carolyn was ill at ease and, without deprecating friendship, wanted to be alone.

'I wish I had a Mrs Mortimer,' Freda said as they ate the delicate sandwiches and drank their tea. 'I shall have to get someone like her when I become a name on Nigel's confinement list. You're booked for god-mother.'

It all sounded so normal and secure, Carolyn thought, and she forced a note of enthusiasm into her voice as she said, 'I'd love that.'

But Freda left the house with a feeling that she had been talking to someone who was not there – a pale ghost hovering in the shadow of yesterday. When she spoke to David, as they sat drinking their cocktails that evening, he advised, 'There isn't anything you can do, darling. Unless I'm very much mistaken the Harrington business is nothing compared with the rest of the trouble. I can see that marriage breaking up.'

'So can I,' Freda said in a low sad voice. Involuntarily, her hand reached out and

David clasped it very tightly...

After evening surgery that night, Carolyn said to Max, 'Come and have a drink. I want to talk to you.' Her voice sounded anxious and she looked upset.

When they were settled, she asked quietly, but directly, 'Is it true that Mr Harrington reported Nigel?'

Max started, took a deep breath, and hoped he did not look as desperate as he felt.

'I don't want evasion, Max. I could not bear it from you.'

'It isn't a question of evasion. This is something you must ask Nigel.'

'You know that Nigel told me that Harrington wasn't reporting you.' There was faint suspicion in her voice. 'Was that his way of telling me a truth in order to hide a deception? I cannot believe that you would allow him to take the blame for something–' She stopped.

Max spoke quietly, 'Not if it were in my power to prevent it.'

Carolyn relaxed a little. 'I think I understand. All this is because of me; because I was involved, and we were out together that night.' She rushed on, 'Now I realise why nothing has been definitely settled, or plans made, for the ending of your association. He wanted the case over first. Even that night when we were supposed to have had a talk about things – it was a waste of time.' Her attitude changed. She finished her drink. 'I know now what is to be done.'

'You mean – us?'

'Yes. I've already said I would like to get away from here, now I want to go away with you when you leave the practice in a few weeks time. It will simplify everything; give Nigel his freedom so that he can continue to practice in the area. I don't like loose ends, or uncertainty. I shan't tell him I know anything about Mr Harrington. That was obviously the way he wanted it and it was a generous gesture. Now it's my turn.' There was a tinge of cynicism in her voice as she added, 'He is fond of secrets; the least I can do is to let him keep this one.'

Max listened in silence, hating his invidious position, yet knowing that it was impossible for him to explain the circumstances. No doubt Freda had mentioned the matter, probably in sympathy. Neither he, nor Nigel, had taken her into account.

'Are you quite sure you are prepared to go through the divorce court as the guilty party? If that is really so, then I had better find somewhere in London where we can live temporarily. The evidence must be fool proof. Then I'd like to take you somewhere in the sun – even if only for a week or two.'

She looked very solemn. 'I'd rather just go away quietly somewhere on my own, once the evidence has been provided. I can always get a job. That is not a problem. Later on, when it was all over, we could be together permanently. I had not thought of that before.'

'And you are going to stop thinking of it now,' he said decisively. 'On your own, indeed. A fine divorce that would be. Deserted before we're even married!' His expression was gentle. 'This is going to be done the right way, Carolyn. The only way.'

She looked down at her hands, unconsciously twisting her wedding ring. A faraway feeling brought unreality.

'I agree,' she said and looked across at him, remembering the dinner by candlelight and the ecstasy of it all. Then, irrelevantly, she exclaimed, 'I hope Anita is genuine–' She paused, a little embarrassed.

'You mean in her love for Nigel?'

'Yes.'

'I don't think you need have any qualms about that. She's in love with him all right. I don't have to approve of her myself in order to realise that. Two doctors... What better?' His voice hardened. Swiftly he added, 'Except us.'

'I shall not discuss any of this with Nigel – I mean mention what we intend to do. The letter left behind may seem melodramatic, but it saves a great deal of unnecessary strain, and has a finality about it.'

'I think I know where I can get just the right small flat,' Max said suddenly. 'A doctor friend has a pretty good practice in Knightsbridge and owns one or two converted houses. He might even be prepared to let me help out in the actual practice.' His expression became thoughtful. 'Strange how life goes in cycles. I nearly went in with him before coming here, but his assistant had about another year to go... As for the letter...!' He looked down into the fire reflectively. 'I agree. Everything we do in life has a touch of melodrama. This would be in a good cause. Would you mind living in London for a while?' he spoke disjointedly his thoughts flashing from one thing to another.

'Of course I wouldn't mind. You are sure Max – about your feelings?'

His smile was tender. 'A little frightened of being so sure. And you?'

'Of course,' she whispered.

'Then there is little else to worry about,' he said firmly. 'Now I must go. Nigel may be back early and–'

She interrupted, 'Has he gone to discuss the case?' Even as she spoke she knew instinctively that he had. 'It doesn't matter,' she hastened. 'Where will you eat?'

'There's stuff in the fridge... If only I could whisk you off for a meal.'

She had a rather forlorn look about her as

he left. The house was like a deserted ruin, with the wind howling mournfully through it as a gale began to blow. She tried to sound cheerful as Mrs Mortimer appeared to inquire about the meal. 'Another of your lovely omelettes,' Carolyn said. 'I shall be afraid to look an egg in the face soon!' She hurried on, 'But I had a very large lunch... Doctor will not be needing anything when he comes in.'

'He would not approve of your eating so little.' There was an anxious note in Mrs Mortimer's voice. 'A little soup first, perhaps.'

Carolyn's stomach revolted at the idea of anything.

'Just the omelette, please.'

'I'd better go quickly before you decide not to have even *that*.'

Nigel came in just before ten o'clock. He looked pale and tired, his face drawn and his expression solemn. The Union had been sympathetic and were taking up his case, but since it was the first complaint he had ever had to deal with in his medical career, the interview had been an ordeal. He was both glad, and sorry, that Carolyn was still downstairs; her presence was bitter sweet.

She tried to re-phrase the 'Can I get you anything?' by suggesting that, as it had turned so bitterly cold, he might like something hot to drink.

He thanked her and poured himself out a whisky. 'Anything happened?'

'Just routine.'

'Freda looks well, doesn't she?' *Freda*. He had forgotten that she might commiserate about the case but, obviously, this was not so, or Carolyn would mention it.

'Wonderfully well; planning to swell your confinement list.' Carolyn tried to sound matter of fact.

Nigel had not sat down. He could not bear Carolyn's nearness, or the intimacy of facing her across the hearth. The memories were too poignant. He gave a half smile which conveyed sadness rather than joy. 'She will have to find herself a new doctor... Goodnight, Carolyn.' With that he went up to bed.

Carolyn followed shortly afterwards. The room had never seemed so lonely or so comfortless. She sat down at her dressing table and began to remove her make-up, seeing her face through blurred vision as the tears welled into her eyes. She dashed them away angrily, but without success. Her body shook with sobs she could not control...

21

It was a fortnight later when Mrs Mortimer came into the sitting-room and said to Carolyn, 'There is a Doctor Benson to see you.'

Carolyn repeated the name, giving a little gasp which she could not suppress.

Anita came in and as the door shut on Mrs Mortimer, said, 'Forgive my intruding, but I had to see you.'

Carolyn looked at her very levelly. Obviously she would know all the facts, therefore the idea of playing the outraged wife – even were she so disposed – would be sheer hypocrisy. She indicated a chair and they sat down. Carolyn's body was tense, her heart beating so fast that it throbbed in her throat. Her mouth was dry. She asked quietly, 'What about?'

'Nigel.'

A silence fell, and in it all the ghosts of memory paraded. Carolyn was baffled and afraid.

'I don't understand. Is anything wrong?'

'Everything.' The note of misery in her voice made Carolyn sympathetic, despite herself. Anita gazed round the room a little helplessly. 'If anyone had told me I'd be here, like this, I should have said they were mad. But I suppose there are limits to living in hell – a time limit. I cannot go on.'

Carolyn's voice cracked. 'You mean with–'

'With Nigel.' She paused. 'Could I have a drink?'

'Of course.' It wasn't real, Carolyn told herself. Anita, the poised, self-assured Anita, sitting there dejectedly. She poured out two Martinis, her hand shaking.

Anita was fighting herself. Fighting against uttering the words she knew had to be uttered, and hating every one of them with a sick, terrifying hatred; yet aware that to go on and be destroyed would lead only to greater wreckage. She sat back further in her chair and sipped her drink. Even the gesture broke a little of the tension. Then, swiftly, the words tumbling out almost involuntarily, she said, 'You see, Nigel doesn't love me and I can't go through with this. I can't live with your ghost for the rest of my life. I thought I could; that I'd make him love me.' She shook her head. 'He can no more love me than I can stop loving him.'

Carolyn shivered. 'You speak of my ghost–'

Anita hastened, 'He has never stopped loving you. Not for a second. No, don't interrupt me, please. I've got to talk to you, make you understand, not just the present, but the past.'

'You were lovers.' The statement was made with all the force of hurt behind them.

'Yes. I came down here determined that we should be so again. I agreed to be co-respondent so that you could divorce him. It was all settled. We were to marry when he was free. I thought I was so happy, even though everything was to spare you. He didn't pretend to me about still being in love with you.' For the first time a note of bitterness crept into her voice. 'Even in these past weeks I've realised how impossible the future would be, and how hard and cynical I should become. I'd be shut away in a world of frustration and hope and anger, knowing that every time he made love to me he would be thinking of you.' She sipped her drink and added, 'I should be no good at that kind of hell, and now is the time to learn my lesson, once and for all. So my being here isn't entirely a noble gesture for his sake; it is a mixture of compassion and self-preservation. A miserable man is an unutterable bore,' she finished fiercely.

Carolyn asked, 'Couldn't you be exaggerating all this?'

'And are you rejecting it because it complicates things with Max? Because you don't want to *believe* that Nigel loves you?'

Carolyn said stubbornly, 'I have no

evidence to substantiate that. Your change of heart–'

'You fool,' Anita cried. 'Should I be here unless it was to convince you?'

That was true, Carolyn argued. She felt that she was standing at the top of a mountain, not daring to believe in the panorama spreading out before her eyes. She tried to keep her hands from shaking; to take deep breaths because she felt suddenly sick.

'If you want to marry Max, that's your business,' Anita went on. 'Nigel will never handicap you; or tell you anything that I am telling you now. He'd hate the idea of making your marriage a responsibility and his love your conscience. You *must* realise that. Nigel doesn't say much, but that doesn't mean he is incapable of deep feeling.'

Colour mounted Carolyn's cheeks. The words struck home and were all the more ironical because Anita used them.

'Nevertheless,' she said defiantly, 'one can get tired of being a thought reader.' She looked at Anita searchingly, 'and of living with secrets. You may appreciate that – since you cannot live with my ghost.' Carolyn dare not weaken; she dare not begin to analyse the emotion that was surging over her, or face up to the truth about her feelings.

'Nigel was such a fool not to tell you about me. But, in fairness, he had no idea that I should ever come back into his life. We're all fools when it comes to the things we choose to conceal.'

Carolyn sighed. Her expression softened.

'It all began,' Anita explained, 'when Nigel, Max and I worked together in the same hospital. Nigel and Max were very great friends – more like brothers, in fact. Max never really liked me, and liked me even less when Nigel and I fell in love.' She paused before adding, 'I'm not going to choose my words, or play anything down. It was the kind of attraction that could have ruined us, and nearly did. Max knew we were lovers, and warned us that there was a dangerous amount of grapevine gossip. But sometimes people have a blind spot.'

Carolyn struggled against the jealousy that tore at her.

'Things came to a head one night when Nigel and I quarrelled. I was half demented. There was an emergency take-in. Perforated ulcer. I gave a transfusion without cross matching the blood. You know what that means.'

Carolyn looked horrified. In all transfusions a drop of the patient's blood, and a drop from a small bottle (hung around the neck of the transfusion bottle, and containing about five millimetres of blood to avoid waste) are cross matched. If the blood clots it is fatal.

Anita's expression was tense, her voice

shaken, as she went on, 'The patient died. Nigel and Max knew the panic-stricken state I was in, and Nigel insisted that he would take the blame.' She made a little helpless gesture as she added, 'But Max realised the danger of any investigation involving either Nigel or me. Our relationship would be brought into disrepute and provide a very unsavoury reason for any mistake, or collusion. Almost before Nigel had time to act, Max accepted full responsibility for the error. A verdict of death from misadventure was returned. Max came in for very severe criticism.' She shivered at the recollection of it all. 'It was a dreadful time. Max tried to make Nigel feel better by reminding him of how much he owed him, and how many scrapes Nigel had seen him through. But it was all very grim. Max left the hospital. All he really wanted was to see me out of Nigel's life. Eventually, I suppose inevitably, we parted, not as enemies, but because the memories were too painful. As time passed I realised how much I still loved him, and traced him here. It didn't matter that he was married.'

Neither spoke for many seconds after those last words died away. They did not look at each other, yet there was no enmity between them. The jealousy and the fear with which Anita had lived so long were like a fire damped almost to extinction.

At last Carolyn asked, 'Does Nigel know you are here?'

Anita shook her head. 'I told him last night that I could not go on with things. But that won't change his view about the divorce. It's been a relief to talk about all this. Thank you for listening. Whatever you decide to do with your life, make quite certain it is the right thing, that's all.'

Carolyn had the strange feeling that she had dreamed the visit as Anita's car drove away. She sat in the firelit room, looking out at the dark tapestry of night through the frame of the windows. It was like watching a film coming back into focus.

The door opened and Max said, 'So Anita came.'

Carolyn turned, speaking breathlessly, 'You knew that she was coming?'

'I asked her to do so. I realised that things could not go on as they have been. Now, I must know the truth about your feelings for me. Are you in love with me – really in love with me?' His gaze was steady and direct.

Carolyn was trembling. She knew just then how greatly she had deceived herself, clinging to Max amid what seemed to be the ruins of her marriage, never daring to look too closely into her heart, or analyse her emotions.

'*Are* you?' He repeated the question.

'No Max.' Her voice was shaken. 'I feel

dreadful, and I'm so very sorry. It would be impossible to explain.'

'And Nigel? It is Nigel – isn't it?'

Colour crept into her cheeks. She hated the hurt behind Max's gentleness, but for the first time for months her body felt that it had been released from a tight torturing harness, as she answered on the breath of a sigh. 'Yes, it is Nigel. It always will be. I can't expect you to understand, or to forgive me.'

'I think I can do both,' he said quietly. 'I was never more than a substitute for Nigel. I was able to give you the emotion you wanted from him. When we are starved of a thing, sooner or later we find it elsewhere.'

'I didn't *realise*,' she exclaimed with emphasis.

'And you never told me you loved me. I used to wait, and I used to watch you. Everything was for Nigel's good. Oh, that isn't a criticism. Far from it. You'd never wanted Nigel's love so much as when you thought you'd lost it. Your concern for him and your anxiety that he should remain here... Everything.'

Carolyn bowed her head, and then her eyes met his in appeal as she admitted, 'I was too confused to recognise the very thing I made so obvious to you.'

His smile was wry. 'People sometimes love

most when they think they have ceased to love.'

'I wish I knew the right thing to say.' She looked bewildered. 'Anita told me everything. If only I'd *known*.'

'I couldn't tell you. I should not have come here, and yet I could never regret doing so, or loving you. Now you understand about the Harrington case. The trouble between Nigel and me is that we both have a great regard and respect for each other. Even despite our loving you. There are so many things in the past I owe to Nigel. I might almost say the fact that I qualified at all.'

'And the things he owes you,' she said quietly. 'I know hospital life and the rigidity of the Powers that Be.'

He nodded and gave a little laugh. 'No sadness, Carolyn.'

'What will you do?' Her voice shook.

'Work abroad for a while. Doctors are good export material.' He lifted her hands and kissed them in turn. 'Be happy,' he whispered, 'and beat that husband of yours over the head if he doesn't behave. Or threaten him with me!' He moved towards the door. 'I'll take over the calls from now on this evening. Keep me occupied... No, stay there,' he said abruptly, and was gone.

Nigel returned that night, weary, disconsolate. Carolyn stood up as he entered the room. He noticed that she was wearing a dress he particularly liked. The neckline shimmered, and had a wide, off the shoulder, effect. She looked transformed.

'I take it,' he said, 'Max stayed to dinner.'

'No; he left after surgery.' She was conscious of Nigel's gaze appraising her, and the thought of all Anita had told her rushed back. It was like standing on the brink of a new love affair, with all its excitement and ecstasy.

'I want to talk to you.' Her eyes looked into his disarmingly.

He sat down in his own chair. It was an involuntary gesture.

'I'm not going to divorce you,' she said firmly 'or be divorced.'

A tremor went over him. He stared at her aghast, aware of her subtle sensuous appeal, and the radiance in her eyes. 'Why?' His voice was breathless.

'Because,' she said simply, 'I love you.'

Emotion creased his face into an expression of amazed disbelief.

'Love me ... *love* me.' His voice broke. 'And Max?'

'He knows and understands. And if you won't talk to me, I must talk to you. Do you love me – really love me, Nigel? I've got to know. Just for once I want *words.*'

'Oh, *darling!* I love you more than I have

ever loved you. It's been utter hell without you.'

She made a little gesture of appeal. 'Why didn't you tell me about things? Anita came here... I know everything,' she said gently.

The relief that betrayed itself in his face brought to the moment a poignancy Carolyn never forgot.

'I'm sorry,' he murmured humbly. 'And so grateful you know. Only Max could have persuaded Anita to tell you the truth.' As Carolyn nodded, Nigel went on, 'It wasn't a question of wanting to deceive you about the past... I didn't profess anything morally, and it never occurred to me that I'd see Anita again. When Max came here I was able to be of some help to him. I intended telling you the whole story. Dr Sims mentioning a partner ... it became an untidy mess. But if you let the right moment pass, things build up. I went from bad to worse. And then, when I believed you were in love with Max, I didn't want to be your conscience.' He paused. 'Knowing all the facts you can realise how I felt. It was not an ordinary situation. The same applied to Harrington.'

'I can understand,' she said fervently. 'Never shut me out again. Never. It does not matter what it is. And I can't live in a cold, detached world. I must make that point. I need to be loved, not just to have a husband who treats me as though I were a piece of furniture, and decries all the normal demonstrations of love.'

He flinched. 'You've every right to say that. It was sheer folly on my part. I was so obsessed with all that was going on...' he broke off apologetically. 'I hadn't the wit to tell you how much you meant to me.' His voice was fierce. 'Or what it meant to sleep in a different room. That was hell.'

The silence was tense and full of memories. She went over to his chair, and knelt on the floor beside him.

'We've both been such fools in our different ways,' she murmured.

His lips went down on hers. He held her, and his arms were like bands of steel. When they drew back for breath, he said, 'I've ached for you, and every damn silly thing I've done has been because I loved you so deeply.' As he spoke he clasped her left hand and fingered her wedding ring. She rested her right arm across his knee. There was a dear familiarity in their nearness.

'You're my husband,' she whispered, softly and significantly.

His gaze lost itself in hers. 'I've never ceased to be your husband, darling. I haven't slept with Anita since she came back into the picture.'

Carolyn's eyes darkened; they were passionate and full of desire. 'I'm glad.'

The clock struck eleven...

Nigel lifted her to her feet. As they went upstairs they were closer than at any time during their marriage.

The bedroom door opened and shut...

The publishers hope that this book has given you enjoyable reading. Large Print Books are especially designed to be as easy to see and hold as possible. If you wish a complete list of our books please ask at your local library or write directly to:

Dales Large Print Books
Magna House, Long Preston,
Skipton, North Yorkshire.
BD23 4ND